D0245006

ÖPIE JONES

JONES

TALKS TO ANIMALS

FOR YASMINE

EGMONT
We bring stories to life

First published in Great Britain in 2021 by
Egmont Books

An imprint of HarperCollins*Publishers*
1 London Bridge Street
London SE1 9GF

egmontbooks.co.uk

HarperCollins*Publishers*
1st Floor, Watermarque Building, Ringsend Road Dublin 4, Ireland

Text copyright © 2021 Nat Luurtsema
Illustrations © 2021 Fay Austin

The moral rights of the author and illustrator have been asserted.
A CIP catalogue record for this title is available from the British Library

ISBN 978-1-4052-9608-3

Printed and bound in Great Britain by CPI Group

1

ÖPIE JONES

TALKS TO ANIMALS

NAT LUURTSEMA

Illustrated by Fay Austin

EGMONT

"I HATE BOOKS THAT START WITH QUOTATIONS."

MARGOT VON CATTON

In this story I come off as a bit bad-tempered.
I am AWARE. You don't need to point it out.
But what you have to remember is, there was
adventure and action and peril, all during a
heatwave.

I am a long-haired cat.

I was UNCOMFORTABLE.

I don't mind being a hero, but someone
should have warned me about the sweatiness.

CHAPTER ONE

THAT MORNING, **OPIE JONES** ATE BREAKFAST WITH A vampire and a NASA astronaut.

Her parents were actors who believed in dressing for the part when they auditioned. "It's professionalism," they would say.

It's the reason the postman doesn't look you in the eye any more, Opie thought but didn't say. She was very polite, so didn't stare as her mother popped out her fangs to eat toast.

"If you worked for NASA would you wear a NASA T-shirt?" Opie's dad, Harvey, was worried. "Or is it a bit Captain Obvious?"

Harvey was Indonesian, a trim, handsome man with unruly eyebrows that he kept in place with a toothbrush covered with hairspray. He'd rather no one knew this, but Opie had once cleaned her teeth with the hairspray-covered toothbrush and his secret had come out, loudly, with lots of spitting.

Opie's mum, Violet, was white, tall and striking with long black hair. She was very funny but she got sad because she didn't work as much as she wanted. Violet was a brilliant actor. She once played a witch on stage and Opie had been so terrified she wet herself. She was three at the time. Ten-year-old Opie handled fear better. Which is good, because scary things were just around the corner.

A year ago Harvey started working on a daytime

show called *Highland Docs*. He played Dr Ahmed, a brooding Ear, Nose and Throat Specialist from Asia. Harvey had asked where in Asia, but the writers couldn't be more specific. So Harvey gave Dr Ahmed an accent that travelled from China to India, and sometimes went to Wales. Violet said whenever you messed up an accent it went to Wales. No one knew why.

Once she'd eaten her porridge, Opie kissed the vampire and the astronaut and headed to school. It was a ten-minute walk and her parents let her go alone. Opie was a very responsible, sensible ten-year-old, and if that makes her sound a bit boring, then fine: she was. But that's why she got to walk to school by herself and more 'exciting' kids did not.

As Opie walked, she felt in the pockets of her dungarees for everything she needed: school ID card, library card, house keys, emergency phone, lip balm.

Opie liked order and routine. She already had a Walking To School routine, with friends she said hello to every morning.

There was the slim older lady who watered her front garden every morning. As Opie passed, the lady was flicking slugs off her precious tomato plants.

"Good morning!" Opie waved and in return got a cherry tomato tossed her way. She discreetly checked it for slug slime before popping it in her mouth.

There was a young police officer who was always leaving his house as Opie was passing and they had got in the habit of giving each other a salute. Once he'd cycled off, Opie stopped by a brick wall and waited a moment.

She checked her watch. *This* friend was always late.

Finally, a gigantic tabby cat with furry tufts on the ends of her ears emerged from a bush and strolled towards Opie, yawning and scattering dry mud. A collar around her neck announced in swirling letters that you were in the presence of Margot Von Catton. Lucky you.

"Come on, I'm going to be late!" Opie said.

Margot never hurried.

She hopped up on to the wall and inspected Opie's hands, checking they were perfectly clean before she allowed her head to be scratched.

Once Margot got bored of her, Opie carried on to school, the sun already hot on the top of her head. She walked down a street dominated by large buildings that gave her some shade and trotted past the Varling cinema, the Varling supermarket and the Varling bowling alley.

Soon she reached the Saint Francis of Assisi school gates. Opie stood in front of her school and sighed. Even being *near* her school made her feel anxious and shy.

Opie had joined the school a year ago, when they'd moved to be near the studio for *Highland Docs*. She was a little quiet in her first week at school. Most people would have been. It was perfectly understandable. But on the Thursday of that first week, a boy called Cillian Keogh had embarrassed her in front of the whole class by saying, "You're really quiet. Is it because you're shy or are you too clever to talk to us?"

Everyone stared at her as Opie blushed a hot red.

"Oh, okay," Cillian said, pointing at her like she was a science experiment. "Shy."

Cillian was an Irish boy with a sweet face that did *not* reflect his personality. Opie had disliked him from that moment. And when, a week later, he started calling her 'Dopey', her dislike hardened into hate.

Thanks to Cillian, her classmates were now convinced she was shy and left her alone. She felt like she had a big sign on her head that said, "SHY! DON'T TALK TO ME PLEASE. SHY!"

Only one person talked to her. Cillian's best friend, Jackson Sato. Jackson was special. He was tall and half-Japanese with dark hair and grey eyes. He was also funny, cool and cheeky. Jackson seemed to glide through life on charm and bending the rules. He never listened properly to anyone, so was unaware of the OPIE IS SHY message.

He couldn't have been more different to Opie, who was hard-working and serious and never bent the rules. She was small and solid, hidden behind long dark hair with a fringe to her nose.

Jackson only chatted to Opie when they were at their lockers, which were next to each other. But at the beginning of term, Cillian came down with mumps.

Opie wouldn't wish mumps on anyone, but it did mean Cillian was off school. She had sat at the back of the class and watched a bored and lonely Jackson fiddle with his hair. At break time she'd wandered over and offered him a crisp. They'd started chatting about his dad's failed attempts to grow potatoes, which had led to the family eating an uncomfortable amount of turnips. This had really made her laugh.

As the days passed, they became friends. Jackson was skilled at making people feel good about themselves. He was never shy about complimenting your brains or shoes or anything in between. Jackson gave Opie confidence and Opie helped Jackson with his schoolwork. (okay fine, she did his schoolwork for him, but it was just quicker that way.) Every morning, Opie anxiously watched the classroom door, expecting Cillian to come in and reclaim his friend, but he was off all week.

On Monday morning, Opie had bounced into school

and stopped dead in the classroom doorway, seeing Cillian and Jackson in their usual seats. But Jackson had spotted her and pulled a chair towards their desks. They had been an awkward three ever since: two frenemies fighting over one charismatic boy.

This was the first problem in Opie Jones's life. The second problem was the strange things that kept happening at her school.

Up until this point, the strangest experience she'd had at Saint Francis of Assisi was when a pigeon had got into assembly. The Deputy Head had run around the hall waving a broom and students got poo in their hair. (Pigeon poo, not Deputy Head poo.)

But in the last couple of weeks, break times had been strange and scary. Kids kept fighting. Sometimes the yard was full of brawling bodies and shoes scattered on the ground. Every time they fought, more of Opie's schoolmates were excluded or expelled. Every week there were more empty chairs in classrooms and kids upset because their friends had gone. It was like an angry plague was running through their school.

Opie started avoiding the yard at break time, preferring to read in an empty classroom. She tried to persuade Jackson and Cillian to join her, but it was not easy in the middle of a heatwave. Especially when she couldn't give them a good reason why.

It was like the *air* was full of rage. She couldn't explain it better than that, and she knew it sounded daft. 'I have a nasty feeling' is not a strong argument. People don't take you seriously. They offer you indigestion tablets.

Opie took a deep breath and headed through the school gates for another day.

Yeah, I'm big into fitness, mate, very big into it. Healthy body, healthy mind. Great stuff.

I eat about three bites of a tomato before that lady chucks me off. Doesn't hurt when I land; I tuck and roll, stay loose, there's a technique. Do all my own stunts.

CHAPTER TWO

OPIE SKIPPED UP THE STAIRS AND INTO SCHOOL, where Jackson was waiting.

To Opie's delight, he was waiting for HER.

Jackson clutched Opie by the shoulders. "OMG – I've been looking for you everywhere!" he gasped and she felt a bit flustered because, honestly, anyone would if Jackson Sato did that to them. He had such nice hair.

"Myerp?" Opie said, ruining the cool moment a bit.

"Marilyn's book report is due today!" Jackson called their teachers by their first names. Not to their faces, but still . . .

"I know," she said. "What book did you do?"

Jackson made a sad noise. "I did NO book!"

"Do you . . . oh, you can't copy mine."

"No, Marilyn knows I copy you now," he moaned.

There was a long silence. Jackson nibbled his hair, sighed and looked anguished.

Opie had a great idea. "We could sit and write it together at break? Maybe best to stay out of the playground anyway, so –"

"We *could,*" said Jackson. "But would I be any help? No, I would not. I'm such a thickie."

"No, you're not!" said Opie sincerely. "I bet you'd be surprised at how well you did if you listened in class and maybe did some work. Just every now and then?"

"Seriously, I'm a goofball. I'll just stay out of your way and give you peace to write it," he whispered, backing away from her on tiptoes.

"Oh, okaaaay," said Opie, realising that she was going to spend her break doing Jackson's homework.

"Hey Opie," Jackson said, flashing her a smile. "You look really stylish today, BTW. So many pockets."

She immediately forgave him.

And so, that break time, she sat in the computer room, working hard on a school laptop. It started to make a whirring noise, complaining about the heat and its workload. Opie felt the same.

A scream from the playground made her jump. She stood and looked out of the window, and was relieved to see it wasn't another fight. It was Jackson screaming as he chased Cillian around the yard. She blew her fringe out of her eyes and sat back down.

Sometimes Opie Jones did not respect herself very much and this was one of those times. She was glad no one knew what she was doing.

"Are you writing Monsieur Sato's book report?" came a voice from the door.

Curses. "Bonjour, Monsieur Lunarca," she said.

Opie liked all her teachers but especially her French teacher, Monsieur Lunarca. He was a small round man who made bold fashion decisions.

"*J'aime bien votre gilet*," Opie told him over the rapid tapping of her laptop.

Monsieur Lunarca stroked his cardigan, which had just got a compliment. "Oh *oui*?" he said, doing that thing you do when you're fishing for a second compliment so you say, "Oh yes?" but in French.

"*Les boutons sont originaux*," Opie said, still tapping.

"The buttons are indeed nice, but don't dodge the question," Monsieur Lunarca said. "You're doing Jackson's work, aren't you?"

"I did offer . . ." Opie said honestly.

Monsieur Lunarca shook his head. "Remember to throw in lots of spelling mistakes and a giddy disregard for grammar, or no one will ever believe he wrote it," he said and left her to it.

Opie grinned and carried on working. She finished just as the bell went, saved the report on a memory stick and then packed up and headed for her locker, where Jackson and Cillian were already getting their books out.

Even though Cillian couldn't do Jackson's homework, he could win his friendship in other ways. His parents had a lot of money and every year his birthday party was a huge event. Cillian would invite the whole class except two or three people, so if you'd been snubbed, you *knew.*

Cillian's next birthday party was a month away. Opie had a nasty feeling that she would be snubbed. She told herself she didn't care, but deep down she did. It's never nice to be left out.

As Opie approached, Cillian was saying, "I think we're gonna book out the whole place, have it to ourselves. There'll be a barbecue and an ice-cream stand. AND we could go early and swim before anyone else gets there!"

"Amazing!! I'd love that!" Jackson grabbed Cillian in a hug, which brought Cillian face-to-face with Opie. Cillian made a smug face at her over Jackson's shoulder.

While they were hugging, Jackson said: "And Opie too?"

Cillian's smile dropped. "Oh hi, Dopey," he said heavily.

Jackson wheeled around, looking pleased to see her.

"Yeah, well," Cillian went on, "maybe. But it's not really her thing, fun." And he gave Opie the classic mean look: a slow down-and-up stare.

"It won't be as fun without Opie," Jackson protested. "You're going to invite her, right?"

Cillian looked like he was chewing a lemon. "I'll have to review the numbers."

"Hurray!" said Jackson.

"Hurray," Opie said flatly. There was no chance Cillian was inviting her to his birthday party. Which, she hated to admit, sounded brilliant.

Jackson tugged on her sleeve. "Um, Opie . . . ?" he said in a cute little voice. "Do you haz my book report?"

Grinning at the funny voice, Opie handed him the memory stick.

"Can I copy that?" Cillian piped up.

Jackson headed for class. "Sure thing, buddy!"

"No, wait, you can't copy!" Opie said.

"I'll change it around a bit," Cillian said with a shrug, pulling his new laptop out of his bag. "All books are a bit samey, right?"

She watched them walk off, packing her bag with irritable roughness. She'd spent all flipping break time writing a book report for someone who was not her friend and thought that all books were a bit sa—

Opie froze. She could hear a little voice . . . singing.

Dum dum daaah. Dum dum daaah.
Duh duh duh –
Duh duh duh,
Duh duh duuh!

A reedy voice was singing a car-insurance advert jingle, though it didn't seem sure of the words. Opie looked up and down the corridor. It was empty. Everyone had gone to class. She could hear a faint scratching, but the only person she could see was her form teacher, Ms Mollo. Outwardly irritable, Ms Mollo was kind deep down. (But like, *very* deep down.)

Opie stared at Ms Mollo.

Duh duh duh duh duh, duh duh spondoliks
da da da da da da da da to Go –

"Yes?" said Ms Mollo, certain she wasn't doing anything to deserve Opie's pained expression.

Dum – daaaaaah!

"Are you okay, Opie?"

"Nothing. Because. Yes, sorry," Opie breathed.

"Come on then, I've got you next." And Ms Mollo shooed her in to the classroom.

Before school and after school. Every day. That's when the small kid with long hair comes to my wall and scratches my head.

So why am I sat here like a chump and my head is NOT BEING SCRATCHED?

I'm gonna push something off a shelf. Hope it smashes.

CHAPTER THREE

OPIE WAS WALKING HOME FROM SCHOOL, ON HER WAY to meet Margot. But as she headed down the street she heard odd noises. Swift whizzing noises, like something thin whipping through the air. She was walking past a park and the noises were definitely coming from there.

Opie paused.

Violet and Harvey were very clear that Opie was to walk straight to school and straight home, or they'd start walking with her again. And Opie would never usually break the rules. But, as she peered through bushes into the park, she heard a new noise.

Someone was crying.

They sounded younger than Opie. Opie glanced around for an adult but there was no one. She hesitated a second, then hurried back to the gate that led into the park. The grass was brown and crunchy after a long hot summer, and the park looked deserted.

Opie was about to turn and leave but she heard the noise again.

Whiiizzzz.

Whiiiiizzzzz flick.

And a quiet, shaky sob.

The noises were coming from a huge clump of bushes. Opie slipped her rucksack off her shoulders and placed it behind a tree, to creep up on whatever was happening. She walked slowly and quietly into the bushes until she was standing behind a tree trunk. She edged her head around the trunk, gradually seeing something that made her feel sick.

There were six kids from her school, four boys and two girls, in the year above. Opie recognised a couple of them. She'd always thought that they were nice. But they were tormenting a boy from the year below her.

The bigger kids were holding long, bendy switches pulled from the bushes, They were slashing them through the air to make whizzing noises. The smaller boy kept his eyes fixed firmly on the switches, flinching when they came too close to him. He was tired and near to tears.

Opie swallowed painfully, her throat dry with fear. "Hey," she whispered.

No one heard. Opie tried to make herself step out from behind the tree she was holding on to, but her feet would not move. Maybe she could run home? She didn't want to be a coward, but she didn't think she was brave enough to confront so many bigger kids. If she ran, maybe she could get Harvey or Violet to come back with her. She might even bump into her policeman friend; his house was closer.

Something shifted in the bushes behind the kids. Opie realised that there *were* adults here. A man in a smart suit and a thin-faced woman with long blonde hair were staring intently at the bullying. The woman was even filming it on her phone. Neither of them were doing anything to help. If anything, they looked pleased.

Opie was disgusted. She straightened up to her full,

small height and took a deep breath, to shout, "HEY!" – loudly this time – when suddenly she felt a hand on her shoulder. The hand squeezed gently, like a silent warning.

Opie froze, closing her mouth. She wanted to look behind her, but she was a little scared of what she'd see.

The older kids suddenly dropped their switches on the dry crunchy grass. They turned to stare at Opie, above her and past her, at whoever was squeezing her shoulder. Looking confused, they apologised and backed away like they didn't know what had happened, leaving just Opie and the shaking boy.

The adults in the bushes were gone. The hand lifted from Opie's shoulder.

Opie finally got up the nerve to glance behind her. She saw nothing, maybe a flash of lilac, but the air was wavy in the afternoon heat and – she rubbed her eyes – she didn't see the lilac again. She picked up the boy's bag from the floor where he'd dropped it. He was embarrassed and scrubbing hard at his face to get rid of the tears.

"Um, well," said Opie gently. "Let's go home."

They headed off down the street, pulling their backpacks on to their shoulders. Opie wasn't usually very good at small talk but she made an effort, as the boy was younger and clearly shaken. His name was Leo. They chatted about school, favourite canteen meals and even the fights in the playground. But something about that reminded her of what had just happened, and maybe Leo felt the same because they both fell silent.

They were passing the house of the tomato-plant lady but she wasn't outside. Leo jumped as Margot leaped on to the wall next to his face. She was a very large cat with an unfriendly face that matched her personality. But she licked Leo's face softly and he closed his eyes, comforted. (Opie had a funny feeling Margot was just enjoying the taste of salty tears. But no reason to ruin a nice moment.)

Margot's rough tongue started to turn Leo's cheek pink.

"Okay, enough. Your face will smell of cat food," Opie said and led him away. Margot watched them

go, looking annoyed. But she always looked annoyed.

Leo ran the final few steps to his front door and Opie stood awkwardly by while he explained his lateness to his mum. It did look like someone had been licking his face. Opie gave Leo's mum her best I-Do-Not-Lick-People's-Faces smile until she accepted his story, and led him inside.

Opie rummaged in her dungaree pockets until she found Violet's old phone, kept for emergencies. She was half an hour late, so this counted as an emergency. She opened the family WhatsApp group.

> **I'm sorry I'm late but I'm coming home!**

> **Are you okay?** her mum replied.

> **There was a kid being bullied.**

> **DID YOU BREAK UP A FIGHT? ATTA GIRL!**

Harvey texted, excitement leaping off the screen. He added some fist emojis.

Opie couldn't honestly say that she had.

> **No but I walked a small crying boy home to his mum.**

> **That's better than breaking up a fight**

her mum said and her dad added lots of heart emojis in agreement.

Now put your phone away and come home,

Harvey said sensibly. And Opie did just that, aiming for the shady bits of the street as she was starting to feel sunburned.

As she walked, she had a funny feeling that she was being watched. She stopped and turned around slowly.

Margot was sitting on a bin, swatting at a fly with a big lazy paw.

Reassured, Opie kept walking. She was now about fifteen minutes from home. She whizzed the zip back and forth on her backpack a few times, to reassure herself. But it sounded unpleasantly like the whizzing noises from those switches and she stopped.

Listen, I don't care what the kid does. But those two were hot on her heels. They were following her, I was sure of it.

I thought about, you know, helping or whatever but it was time for my nap. I need five a day or I can get a little grumpy.

CHAPTER FOUR

O PIE GLANCED BACK. SHE THOUGHT SHE SAW A FLASH of lilac again but . . . maybe not. She did have a long fringe that her cycling proficiency teacher called "dangerously obscuring".

She was starting to feel prickles of danger. If you want to understand this feeling, take a big bag of chips down to the seaside, sit near a flock of seagulls and . . . well, good luck with that and all the best with your recovery.

Opie was not being followed by a massive seagull. So that was something.

She was being followed by a man and a woman.

The woman was black, teacher-aged and dressed for business head-to-ankle. From the ankle down, she was wearing high-heeled glittery boots.

The man was younger, white, with dramatic cheekbones and an even more dramatic dress sense. He was wearing a lilac cape.

Opie could hear their footsteps getting closer. They sounded loud, two sets of high heels clattering on the cobbles. She didn't look back. She just ran, with her heavy, bouncing backpack threatening to unbalance her with every step.

She wished *Things* would stop happening to her today. She just wanted to go home and eat a jacket potato.

Opie darted down an alleyway beside the Varling cinema. It was cool; the tall buildings blocked out all the sunshine. Opie appreciated the temperature but not the spooky atmosphere.

She soon outpaced the strangers and could hear their clattering footsteps getting quieter. After a few minutes she felt safer and slowed to catch her breath, careful not to pant too loudly. She was almost home. She scrabbled in her pocket for her phone again, pressed the number 9 twice, then kept her thumb hovering over the 9 so she could call the emergency services in a heartbeat. (Opie Jones was a very smart girl.) She turned the corner –

And came face to face with the strangers, standing there, waiting for her. Smiling.

Opie squeaked with fear and dropped her phone. (Okay, not like *genius* smart.)

The man held up his hand.

Calm.

The word popped into Opie's head and with it a feeling like a cool breeze, blowing away all her worries and all her thoughts. She stood, mouth open, eyes unfocused for a second. She was so dazed, she took a step backwards, wobbling on legs that felt borrowed, and fell over a bin. She landed hard on her bum, and the warmth and noise returned to her head.

"Stop it." The woman slapped the man's hand down in a big sisterly way. Then she turned to Opie and smiled. Opie did not smile back.

"You're Opie aren't you?" the woman began. "You're very special, you have a g–"

"No, I'm not," said Opie. "Special."

"I wasn't finished." The woman looked annoyed. "I have a whole thing I say."

"We do a thing." The man swooshed his cape dramatically. "You are *sooo* very special."

"I haven't got there yet!" The woman was annoyed at

both of them now. "Don't do a silly voice. It's important!"

"How do you know my name?" Opie asked.

"We've been watching you."

The woman twinkled.

Opie didn't twinkle back. "Well, that's a creepy thing to say to someone," she said.

The woman was firm. "We're doing it in a professional way, this is a professional –"

"– operation, sorta thing," the man added.

Opie scrabbled on the ground for her phone. She was still nervous and the adults exchanged a guilty look.

"Don't be scared. Is it the cape?" the man said. "Is it too much? Be honest. I love it but maybe it's not for work. I could keep it for brunches."

"My name's Mulaki. This is Xu," the woman said, talking over Xu, who was fussing about *maybe a jumpsuit would give the same impact, but not be so 'extra'?* "Opie, you have a gift."

"Um, how do you spell . . . ?" Opie asked, struggling to keep up with all this new information.

"G – I – F – T?" Mulaki said.

Opie sighed and shook her head.

"X – U," Mulaki said, pointing at her colleague. "And I'm M – U – L – A – K – I."

"Good for Scrabble," Opie said. "If proper nouns were allowed, which I know they aren't but some people relax the rules at Christmas or Hanukkah for example." She was babbling to calm her nerves. It wasn't working.

"Oh. Pee." Mulaki separated Opie's name into two irritable sounds. "You have a gift. But you already know that."

Honestly, Opie did NOT already know that. She did well in exams but that was because she paid attention in class, which was hardly worth chasing someone down an alleyway in high heels on a hot day for. ("Excuse me! – *pant, gasp* – You concentrate really well!")

"That's why you were at the park just now," Mulaki said. "You heard the bullying."

"Yeah, I heard it. I have ears."

"No . . ." Mulaki shook her head, smiling. "You *heard* it." And she pointed at her head.

"Yes," said Opie patiently, pointing at *her* head.

"With my EARS. Right here."

"Oh god, I'm bored," sighed Xu. "Listen, Opie Jones, you are a mind reader. A special, unique, superhuman freak in a beautiful way." He held out his hand towards her. His cape flapped gently and he looked like a wizard. "Now, can you stop being such a wally? We'll be here all night and you live in a rough area, no offence."

"I . . . what?" spluttered Opie. "I can't read minds. I'm not special, I'm boring. I like all types of music, I eat ready-salted crisps and I think rules are there for a reason. You've got the wrong person, sorry."

"Wow. That is pretty dull," said Xu, suddenly sounding less certain.

"Honey, we're not going to *hurt* you," Mulaki said.

Opie turned on her heel, darted out of the alleyway and pelted towards the safety of home.

Xu gave his boss a hard stare. "We're not going to *hurt* you?"

"Oh shut up."

Mulaki set off after Opie again. Xu followed her at an

elegant trot, shouting, "How about 'we're not going to kill you and pickle your head?' Really reassure her."

Opie was running as fast as she could, but the adults were gaining on her. It was impossible to lose them, like they were predicting her zigzagging route. Luckily, Opie's brain was faster than her feet. So when she reached the main road, she stopped by a line of parked cars.

"Opie?" Mulaki called softly. "We don't want to scare you . . ."

"Then stop chasing me!" Opie shouted back. Which was an excellent point.

"We have to talk to you, it's important!"

Mulaki was using a very teacherly tone of voice, as if Opie had disappointed her. Opie couldn't bear that tone of voice. She checked her watch. She was now nearly an hour late.

Mulaki and Xu were out of breath but clearly poised to follow her again. Opie darted towards a parked car and yanked at its door handle. Immediately, the alarm started to wail. She hurried along a line of parked cars, flapping all their handles until there was a chorus of *Ooooweeeeeee ooooooo weeeeeeee waaaaaah waaaaaaaah*. Curtains twitched and doors opened in the houses along the road.

Xu and Mulaki froze, then spun around and started strolling in the opposite direction, hands in their pockets, whistling softly. Just two pals off on a summer evening's walk. Not chasing anyone. Certainly not stealing cars.

Opie darted round a house and peeked back at them. She could see Mulaki folding her long body into the driver's seat of an old sports car, a pearly white vehicle with black details. Xu was drawing something on the pavement with chalk, contorting himself to make sure his cape didn't drag on the floor. Three brisk lines and he was done.

He hopped into the passenger seat of the sports car and Mulaki accelerated away.

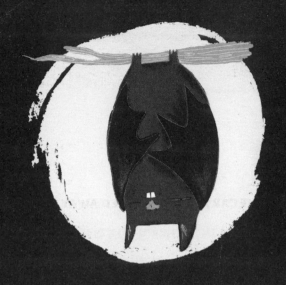

Don't mind me. Just trying to sleep. Absolutely love snoozing while ten car alarms go off. Good thing I don't have super-sensitive hearing.

CHAPTER FIVE

THE WAIL OF CAR ALARMS DRIFTED AWAY BEHIND **O**PIE.
Soon all she could hear was her own panting and
the slap of her trainers on the ground. She hoped she
didn't run past anyone from school because she
looked like a bit of a dope: red-faced, sweaty, running
half-bent with a stitch in her side.

Home was a ground-floor flat in a tower block. She
scrambled her keys into the door, hurried into the flat
and around the corner of the living room.

"Are you okay, sweets? Who was being bullied?"
Harvey said, pausing the TV.

Opie made a quick decision. She would not tell her
parents anything about Mulaki and Xu. She loved
walking alone to school, and if she told her parents
she was being chased by weirdos they would definitely

start chaperoning her again. And she didn't think those two were dangerous. Odd, but not dangerous.

"Sorry I'm late," she panted. "It was just some kids from school."

"Just so long as you're safe," said Violet. She stroked Opie's face with cool, soft hands and Opie felt very safe actually. "Brave girl. Gosh, you're warm."

"It's still hot out," said Opie, squirming a little. She never lied to her parents. It felt gross.

"I've had a jacket potato in the oven for the whole of *Lord of The Rings*," Harvey said, pointing at the TV, "so it should be lovely and fluffy inside."

"The WHOLE of *Lord of The Rings*?" Violet asked. "The trilogy? It'll be a flaming ball of ash."

"No, just *The Fellowship*."

Opie retrieved her jacket potato from the oven. She didn't know why she'd thought her parents would be cross with her. They were so laid back, she could count on one hand the number of times she'd been told off. One hand wearing a mitten.

Opie's mum was tapping busily on her laptop at the dining table. Violet had set Harvey up on social media so that he could talk to his fans, but he received romantic messages that made him shy. So Violet took over and replied as Dr Ahmed.

"This woman wants you to come and live with her in her penthouse in Chelsea, Harv!" Violet called over.

"No thanks, I don't like heights."

"Hmm." Violet hovered her fingers over the keys. "I will tell her you would love to sweep her off her feet but you have a waxy ear to cure and medicine will always be your first love."

"Tell her you'd sweep her off her feet in a smooth motion, so there is no risk of twisting her ankle," Opie suggested, sitting down at the table with her mum. "Sounds more doctorly."

"That's good." Violet was impressed. "And this man wants to know if your grey hairs are highlights or natural, Harvey?"

Harvey laughed. "I don't have grey hairs! . . . Do I?" He hurried off to the bathroom. A second later he wailed, "I've got grey hairs! Why did no one *tell* me?"

Violet shrugged as Harvey returned to stare accusingly at his family. "I'm sorry, I assumed you knew what was happening *on your own head.* So . . . *Thank you for your interest,*" Violet read aloud as she tapped out the answer on her computer. "*The grey hairs are natural and come from the stress of being a doctor.*"

Harvey, tongue poking out in concentration, pulled a long grey hair from the front of his head. "Pluck one grey hair and seven come to its funeral," Violet warned, and he stopped.

"Can you hear that?" Opie asked, pointing outside the window.

Her parents looked in the direction she was pointing.

"Traffic?" Harvey guessed.

"A plane?" offered Violet.

"No, it's . . . shouting," Opie murmured and moved towards the window.

"Probably just someone singing badly. You're lucky to live with people with perfect pitch. I can give you a middle C, right now, not even thinking about it," said Harvey airily.

Opie wasn't convinced, she was sure someone out there was shouting about... moths?

Feeling tired, Opie headed to her room. It was full of books: on the floor in tidy piles, alphabetised along home-made shelves and on top of her wardrobe. She got ready for bed, putting on her pyjamas and plaiting her hair to stop it tangling. It was still warm out so she opened her windows wide to let a breeze in.

Opie closed her eyes and enjoyed the cool air – but her eyes snapped open as she heard a deep, rasping voice.

Where are you? I'm hungry.

Opie froze, gripping the curtains. Not daring to move, she slid her eyeballs left and right. There was no one and nothing but two large oak trees, the branches looming close to her windows.

A leaf rustled and Opie's nerve broke. She drew the curtains tightly and backed away from the window.

No don't. You'll tease me and I'm already embarrassed about it.

I'm scared of the dark.

I know! I'm a badger! I'm nocturnal! It's so lol. Don't even.

There's ghosts and robbers and all sorts in the dark. Moths! So scared of moths. What if one went in my ear and FLUTTERED? I. Would. Die.

I get my food bits during the day. You just have to be organised.

CHAPTER SIX

OPIE WAS WRAPPED IN HER DUVET DESPITE THE HEAT, with a big pair of headphones clamped to her head. Even with the window closed she could hear that rasping voice saying it was looking for dinner. The way it said that made it clear that dinner was not a jacket potato but would involve some running and screaming.

Opie did not feel brave enough for this.

She decided to concentrate on something else, like at the dentist when she counted ceiling tiles to distract herself from the grinding noises. Opie rummaged through her bedside table until she found a half-plaited friendship bracelet. She looped one end over her big toe with shaky hands and concentrated on plaiting it.

Suddenly she heard a new voice. A small, frantic-sounding voice.

It's coming!

Run.

Faster faster faster fa–

She turned and stared out of her window. *Who* was out there?

Something grabbed her foot and Opie screamed and flailed, aiming weak punches at the air.

"All right, sweets?" Violet said, baffled.

"Yeah! Yeah, good," Opie lied, fumbling the headphones off one ear.

"Are you making a friendship bracelet?"

"Wha – uh – gah. Yeah."

The voices went quiet as Opie wiped her forehead with a cold hand and concentrated on her mum.

"Who's it for?"

"Um. Is it weird to make a friendship bracelet for someone you *want* to be your friend? I mean, maybe they're your friend but it's not like . . . definite."

"No," Violet assured her. "It's a confident thing to do. And those are good colours, Jackson will love it."

Opie examined the bracelet, unsure if she was the

sort of person who did a 'confident' thing.

"Wear it yourself. And if he likes it, say, 'Oh, it's just, like, a friendship bracelet, have it if you want, whatever, it's cool'." Violet did a good impression of her daughter's mumbling way of speaking. Parents who went to drama school were a blessing and a curse.

"I don't sound like that," Opie said firmly.

"Of course not, cherub." Violet kissed her forehead. "Oof. You're hot. Let me open a window –"

"No!" Opie cried. "No, I . . . it gets noisy."

"Does it?" Violet looked out of the window at the deserted patch of grass, shrugged and left.

As soon as Opie was alone, the voices surged back into her head, so she focused on plaiting the bracelet again. She finally nodded off at four in the morning, with a complicated friendship bracelet hanging off her toe. If she had to do that every night, she'd have hundreds of friendship bracelets and no one to give them to. She couldn't imagine the look on Cillian's face if she tried to tie one on him. He'd probably chew his arm off.

Opie hurried to the bathroom for a wash, while her

dad's face smouldered at her from the back of the door. Violet was proud of *Highland Docs* and had framed posters of Dr Ahmed around the flat. Opie's least favourite was the one in the bathroom that stared at you while you were on the toilet. No one wants that.

Harvey promised Opie the experience was worse for him.

I can't talk right now. Busy burying stuff
for winter.

Nuts mainly. But also things to cheer
me up in winter.

Like Lego men, it's nice to dig them up,
see old friends.

CHAPTER SEVEN

OPIE HURRIED INTO HER FIRST CLASS OF THE DAY, A little late, and stopped in the doorway, confused. Ms Mollo bumped into her back with a noise of annoyance.

"Sorry. Ms Mollo . . . where is everyone?" Opie said.

A third of the class was missing.

Ms Mollo consulted the register. "Katie, Ross, Evelyn and the three Chrises have been excluded for fighting in the playground yesterday. Robert and Sam were suspended for fighting in the lunch hall, Jamie and Bo had a (very quiet) punch-up in the library after school and Chloe told the Head to . . . ah."

"She told her to *get stuffed*!" Jackson said helpfully.

"Yes, thank you, Mr Sato," said Ms Mollo. "I was refraining from using such language in front of the class."

"I know much ruder words," said a boy at the front.

Hands went up around the classroom from pupils keen to join in.

"If you tell me ANY of the rude words you know," said Ms Mollo crisply, "I will hand out detentions and this class will get even smaller."

Kids lowered their hands, disappointed.

As the class was so small, everyone had to pay attention. Except Jackson. Whenever Ms Mollo asked him a question he said "No thank you" very politely, like she'd just offered him a cupcake and he was full.

Monsieur Lunarca once said Jackson's main contribution to school was as a decorative feature. Jackson was delighted by that.

As everyone set to work, Opie looked over at Lottie and Amit, who sat near her. They were best friends with Evelyn and, now she was excluded, there was an empty chair between them.

Opie tore a piece of paper out of her notebook, rolled it up and flicked it at them, hitting Amit behind the ear harder than she'd intended. He turned around, scowling and rubbing his neck.

"Sorry," she mouthed. "What happened to Evelyn?"

Amit shrugged and offered no explanation. Opie looked at Lottie and raised her eyebrows.

Lottie glanced carefully at Ms Mollo before replying. She started mouthing words carefully and silently. Several members of the class listened in, curious.

"We were playing the, you know that game with the chalk and the –"

"No but never mind," Opie mouthed, keen to get to the important bit.

"Right. So, playing that and she suddenly went . . ." Lottie struggled to explain it and waved her open hand back and forth in front of her face.

"Blank? Unfocused? Distracted?" offered Opie, who had a very big vocabulary.

Lottie nodded. "Then she got up . . ." Lottie's eyes were fixed on Ms Mollo, who was moving around the room checking people's work, ". . . and just *ran* into a group of people. Knocked them flying. Some of them got up, shoved her, she shoved back and then . . ." Lottie bounced her hands in the air as if she was patting an invisible ball.

Opie got it: a huge brawl of kids.

Ms Mollo worked her way towards them and all the kids who were listening to Lottie quickly turned back to their work.

Later, as everyone streamed to the lunch hall, Opie grabbed her packed lunch and sneaked off to the library. She had important research to do. She spent an hour patiently trawling through online articles, reading about mind readers. There was nothing very scientific and she ended up on a lot of homemade-looking websites with gifs of ghosts.

Opie *was* hearing voices, but they were nothing like when Xu pushed that word 'calm' into her head and she became calm. Her voices seemed . . . different.

As she worked, she fiddled with her friendship bracelet.

Suddenly Cillian appeared behind her and peered at her laptop screen. "Dopey! Why are you googling ghosts?"

"Shush, I'm not."

"You are." He pointed, leaving a greasy dot on the screen. "Have you got ghosts?"

There was a shush from behind one of the bookcases. "Sorry," Opie whispered and got shushed for THAT too.

Jackson followed Cillian into Opie's reading nook. "What's that?" he asked, pointing at the friendship bracelet round her wrist.

Opie put her mum's advice into practice. "Nothing, just a friendship bracelet thing." She slipped it off. "You can have it if you want, whatever, I don't mind or . . ."

"Ooh. Cool!" Jackson tied the bracelet on to his wrist, delighted.

Cillian was not happy. "My little cousin makes them," he said.

"That's a really interesting story, thank you, Cillian. I think we all got something out of that," Opie said fake-sincerely and Jackson stifled a giggle. Cillian did not bring out Opie's nicest side and vice versa.

"Yeah . . . you know how she makes them?" Cillian went on. "She winds the thread round her big toe. Is that how you do it, Dopey?"

Jackson looked horrified. "No. Is it? Opie, I hate feet!"

Jackson did hate feet, of course, Opie knew that; he had hated feet ever since an uncle with long toenails stayed for Christmas and walked around barefoot. In protest, Jackson pitched a tent in the back garden and had to be carried in when it snowed. Opie could have kicked herself for walking into that trap.

Jackson was panicking now, tugging at the bracelet but only making the knot tighter. And Cillian was freaking him out.

"Is that what you do? Wind the thread around your big toe and pull it tight into the cheesy skin, maybe when you've been walking barefoot in the bathroom?" Cillian asked Opie, hand on his chin with an innocent, interested look on his face.

Jackson held his wrist out to them. "Get it off NOW or I will be sick," he announced. There was another shush from the depths of the library. "No. YOU shush!" he cried across the room. "I am having a terrible experience!"

With a satisfied look at Opie, Cillian ripped the friendship bracelet off Jackson's wrist and tossed it at her.

"I'm sorry, Opie," Jackson said, scrubbing his wrist with his jumper hem. "If it touched your foot, it just makes me want to puke!"

"Ew, gross, your foot," Cillian whispered cattily. "Gross."

The bell rang and the few people in the library headed back to class. Embarrassed, Opie swept the broken friendship bracelet into the bin as she left.

I struggle in class. Cos . . . look at me! Thousands of eyes. I get distracted very easily.

I'll be all, "Henry the Eighth liked a wedding, did he? Tell me more, Miss!" and the next second: "WHAT'S THAT SHINY THING?"

There was a bit of tinfoil near our school once – sunny day, big unit, really sparkling. We couldn't get a thing done 'til a bigger kid was sent out to bury it.

CHAPTER EIGHT

THE LAST LESSON OF THE DAY WAS GEOGRAPHY. **I**T WAS hot and the air in the classroom was stale. Opie sat by the open window. She'd only had a few hours' sleep last night and was feeling groggy.

She hid a yawn – then suddenly snapped her head up, extremely alert. "Sorry, Ms Mollo, what?"

Ms Mollo took her glasses off and looked at Opie. "Your essay on rocks, Opie. On my desk."

Opie had completely forgotten about that essay. She'd meant to do it last night but forgot in all the drama. This was not like her.

"Ms Mollo, I'm sorry, can I please bring it to you –"

"No Opie, now or never. "

"I can do it in an hour after school. One hour and I'll have it on your desk."

"You can't write an essay in an hour, Opie," Ms Mollo sighed.

"Yes, I can, I do, I will!" Opie blurted out.

She was panicking at the thought of a zero mark. She had never got lower than nine and a half out of ten, and *that* was when she had chicken pox and took the test from home. But as soon as she could, she'd wrapped a scarf around her face and gone to school anyway, keen to not miss out.

It was a sign of how nice Opie's school was that no one made fun of her for being such a swot. Cillian rolled his eyes but Opie didn't see. She was too busy looking at the classroom door.

She now had a bigger problem than rocks.

Mulaki was staring at her through the glass door. To her horror, the handle on the door started turning.

"No no no . . ." Opie shook her head frantically, but Mulaki ignored her and walked in.

The room fell silent.

Opie put her hand up to ask a question, trying to

distract her teacher. Ms Mollo gazed past her, eyes unfocused. Opie waved her hand a little at her teacher.

No response.

"You'll be waiting a while," Mulaki told her.

Opie looked around at the rest of the class. They weren't moving; some kids were frozen mid-gesture. The only movement they were making was blinking.

It was eerie – and then it got worse. On some silent invisible command, all the pupils stood and filed out of the room, followed by Ms Mollo.

"Um, Jackson?" Opie called after her friend. Not a flicker of a response. "Cillian?" But he didn't look round either. Maybe for the best, she thought. Imagine if she couldn't talk to anyone except Cillian. Bleurgh.

Only Mulaki and Opie were left behind. Mulaki shut the door and perched on Ms Mollo's desk, twinkling smugly at Opie.

"Remember me? G-I-F-T?" she said.

"G-o space a-w-a-y," said Opie.

MULAKI
Sorry I can't.

Her lips didn't move; the words just appeared in Opie's head.

Opie stiffened and shouted, "BLAGH!" (No, that's not a word, but it's hard to think when someone appears *in* your head.) She rubbed her eyes hard and hoped when she opened them Mulaki would be gone.

But Mulaki was still there.

"Opie, I want to help you," she said.

"Have you got an essay on rocks?" said Opie. "That would really help."

"How about a good night's sleep? You look like you didn't sleep well. Were you hearing voices?"

"Yes," Opie finally admitted.

Mulaki nodded. "Of course you are. You're a mind reader, Opie. You're reading minds."

"I'm . . . what?"

Mulaki spread her hands like, *Surprise!*

Opie WAS surprised.

"So I am hearing people's *thoughts*? Do they know?" she asked.

"They've no idea," said Mulaki. "You're basically a superhero, NBD mate. So do you want to join us?"

"Who is *us*? Wait. Who ARE us. No." (Opie was excited. But grammar is important.)

Mulaki drew a capital R on the white board with two rapid strokes.

"The Resistance," she said mysteriously.

MULAKI
OOₒₒₒOₒOOₒₒₒ

Opie batted at her ear. "I don't know what The Resistance is, so there's no point doing spooky noises in my head."

"Fine." Mulaki got comfortable, like she was about to tell a story. "There's a man called Varling."

"I know him!" said Opie. "He bought the library and turned it into shops. He owns the cinema and the bowling alley and the supermarket now. He puts his name on all his buildings."

"He wants this school now. To turn into a warehouse."

"Sorry, *what*?" Opie was horrified.

"AND he wants Saint Francis students to work in it.

He thinks the state shouldn't pay for kids to "loll around in school" until they're sixteen –"

"We don't loll! I work hard!"

"I know, I agree!" Mulaki held up her hands. "The Resistance is trying to stop him. Will you help us?"

Opie nodded enthusiastically. This was the most exciting thing to ever happen in double Geography – a competition that was easy to win.

Mulaki shook Opie's hand. "I'll pick you up at noon tomorrow."

"To do what?"

But Mulaki was already halfway out the door. Opie heard her heels walking away. She waited for the sound to grow faint, because she liked Mulaki but was still quite scared of her.

Then she peeped out of the classroom door and felt more scared. Ms Mollo and the class were standing in the corridor in a tightly packed group, facing the wall. Mulaki had tidied them away like PE equipment.

Opie glanced up and down the corridor. If anyone found them like this, she would not be able to explain it. The world's worst, most sinister game of hide-and-seek?

Opie suddenly flattened herself against the wall as the whole class, as one, turned to face her. None of them looked at her. They stared dead ahead and filed back into the classroom in silence. They sat down and, after a second, the normal classroom hubbub started again.

Ms Mollo took her place at the front of the class. "First thing Monday morning," she said dreamily. Her eyes were unfocused. "On my desk, your essay on rocks, Opie."

"Oh good, thank you, that's . . . thank you." said Opie, highly creeped out.

So I'm a woodlouse. But people call me loads of different names . . . it depends where they live.

They call me nutbug, billy buttons, cheeselog, cheesy bug (I don't smell cheesy, that is rude), monkey pea, chicky pig . . . gramfy croojer?!

No one ever asks me my *name* name. It's Jasmin.

CHAPTER NINE

IN THE SUMMER TERM, THERE WAS REAL EXCITEMENT AT the end of every day. Kids raced out of school, bags banging on their backs, hands stretched in front of them. If they hurried they could get an hour of sunshine in the park. If you Photoshopped an erupting volcano behind them, it would look appropriate.

Opie followed slowly behind Jackson and Cillian, lost in thought, until she heard her name mentioned. She looked up.

"Cillian says you won't fit in his mum's car," said Jackson. "Is that okay, Opie? She's giving us a lift."

"It's not small," Cillian was keen to point out. "It's a sports car."

"Aren't there two seats in the front and two in the back?" Jackson said, puzzled.

"Mmm, it's a *weight* thing as much as a size thing, so . . ."

"That's all right," said Opie. "I usually walk."

Cillian's mum, Liz, was waving at them in the car park.

"Hello Opie!" she said. "How's your dad? I couldn't believe Connor and Poppy are actually twins. I never saw that coming! Because she dyes her hair blonde, they look so different. I think Poppy has feelings for Dr Ahmed too though, don't you think? When she was crying in the consulting room and their hands touched over that vomit bowl, the atmosphere was electric!"

Liz was a big *Highland Docs* fan. Opie thought she might also have a Dr Ahmed poster in the bathroom.

"I'll ask Dad if he knows anything," she said.

"Thank you! Have you got your invite to Cillian's pa–"

"*Mother*," said Cillian firmly, waggling his eyebrows at her.

"Oh, okay," said his mum, looking awkward. "Well, um, better head off, boys. Do you want a lift, Opie?"

"No she doesn't, she's fine, loves a walk," said

Cillian, bundling Jackson into the car.

Opie gave Jackson a little wave and headed home, feeling lonely.

Back at home, Opie found her mother was in a bad mood too.

"Opie!" Violet shouted when she heard the door open. "My audition went HORRIBLY. I told them I really connected with the despair and self-loathing of the character and they did not like that! So I got ice lollies for dinner!"

"It's an investment really, in this weather," Harvey chipped in supportively.

Opie froze. She could hear a voice in her head. Either her mum or her dad were thinking . . .

Dun Dun Dun Dunnn Dunnnnnnnnn Dun Dun Dun Dunnnnnnn Dun Dun Dun Dun.

"Um . . ." Opie popped her head into the living room. "Did one of you watch *Star Wars* today?"

Violet did finger guns at her. "Pew pew pewpewpewpew!"

So Opie could read her mother's mind and it was a surprisingly simple place. Well, good for her. Opie's brain was a busy and complex place and she'd swap it for *"Dun Dun Dun Dunnn Dunnnnnnnnn"* right now.

Opie grabbed an ice lolly from the freezer, squeezed next to her parents on the sofa and turned the volume up on the television, hoping this would drown out the sound of her parents' thoughts.

The next morning, Opie woke up on the sofa, leaning against her mum. Harvey was curled into the armchair in the corner of the room. She checked her watch. Nearly ten o'clock. Jackson had once said if you combined the money of Cillian's parents, the cooking of his and the lack of rules at Opie's house, you'd have the perfect home life. Perhaps it was true.

Opie washed and dressed, not sure how to look for her mysterious meeting with Mulaki at noon. She went for an outfit with a lot of pockets, because there was no situation where pockets weren't useful.

Violet and Harvey were going shopping that morning. Opie tried to hurry them out of the door before Mulaki turned up, but they were both faffing in front of the mirror, pulling at their faces and bodies, declaring themselves 'haggard wrecks'.

Harvey turned sideways in front of the mirror and admired his flat belly. Violet tickled him until he stopped holding his breath. His stomach resumed its normal position, hanging slightly over his belt like it was talking to his shoes.

Opie stood by the front door, shaking a jacket hopefully at her mum.

"I'm not a bull, Opie," Violet said, and wandered into the kitchen for another cup of tea.

Opie checked her watch. Noon already. Through the thick wavy glass in the front door, she could see the distinctive outlines of Mulaki and Xu. It looked like Xu was wearing a tiara.

She opened the door. Xu *was* wearing a tiara.

"Well hello, dull girl!" Xu chirped.

"Hello," Opie replied, annoyed at herself for that dull reply.

"Opie? Who's that?" Violet called from the kitchen. Her parents came to join her in the hallway.

"You must be Opie's sister." Xu twinkled at Violet, who was instantly charmed. Then he turned a captivating smile on to Harvey. "We're Opie's friends."

Harvey frowned. "You're my ten-year-old daughter's friends?" he asked. "Friends from work, or from her time in the army?"

"Oh, whatever," said Xu. He waved his hand at Harvey and Violet. They immediately looked blank.

"Have a lovely time at Hula Hoop Academy, Opie," said Violet in a dreamy voice.

Harvey kissed her on the back of the head. "Bye bye."

"Come on then!" Xu said.

Opie didn't move. "Sorry, no," she said. "Look at the state of my parents. If you leave them like this they'll wander into traffic."

Ten minutes later, Xu, Mulaki, Violet, Harvey and Opie were sitting in the living room. Mulaki made Harvey and Violet a sweet cup of tea each, and as they sipped it they looked less blank. Mulaki explained that Opie had been enrolled in a summer club for studious kids who preferred books to sunshine. (Opie scowled at this description of herself, but her parents nodded like, *Yes, that's her. Accurate.*)

"Call if you need anything, Opie," said Violet at last. She kissed Opie goodbye. "Drink lots of water, it's very hot out."

"Nice to meet you, Moo and Zoolaki." Harvey still seemed befuddled.

As Opie left with Xu and Mulaki, she shook her head at Xu.

"What?" Xu protested.

"You know full well what," Mulaki said as they walked to the car.

"I just think whatever you did was a bit overkill on my dad," Opie grumbled. She stopped at the sight of Mulaki's sports car, gleaming like a pearl in the bright sunshine. It was beautiful. "Shotgun?" Opie said, hopefully.

Xu laughed. "No way. You're not even a full member yet. Back seat for you."

Gosh.

                            Yeah, I know.

Thought it would be nice
to have a COUPLE of kids.

                                   Yeah.

This is overwhelming. There's
like, a hundred of them. Do you
know a hundred names?

                          Um. I like Mary?

Mary 2, Return of the Mary,
The Mary and the Maryer . . .

                           Mary: Endgame.

CHAPTER TEN

MULAKI DROVE FOR TWENTY MINUTES, LONGER THAN Opie had anticipated. She didn't recognise anything out of the window. It was all trees and greenery. Opie was a city kid; she felt like they'd gone to a different planet.

Mulaki eventually pulled in next to a huge park, and Xu got out and headed into the long grass, disappearing from view. Mulaki followed, looking around, as if trying to find someone. This was all very suspicious and Opie was glad she had her phone.

Although, how would *that* 999 call go? "Help, I am with two mind readers. That's right, mind readers. Snazzy dressers, no manners. Police and a fire engine please."

The park was big and wild, full of ancient oak trees;

nothing like the little parks near Opie's house, with patchy grass and dog poo bags dangling off trees like disgusting Christmas baubles. The grass was dry from the heatwave and so tall it reached Xu's waist. Opie was much shorter and struggled to wade through it, spluttering as the seed heads hit her in the mouth.

Opie spat out bits of grass while Mulaki and Xu stood still, looking like they were smelling the air. Everything was quiet, apart from the faint background roar of cars. Mulaki pointed decisively in one direction and set off. Xu followed without a word. Opie trooped behind them, fighting her way through more grass, unable to see more than a foot in front of her, until –

"Erk!" She stumbled upon a person sitting cross-legged on the ground, toppled over his shoulder and landed upside down with her head in a molehill.

Mulaki pointed at a nineteen-year-old young black man, serious and stocky in a Varling Cinema polo shirt. "This is Troy."

"Good afternoon," Opie said, knocking mud out of her hair.

"And you . . . fell over Bear."

Bear was a thirty-year-old Indian man, who was chewing green bubblegum and wearing a Jurassic Park t-shirt. He blew a gum bubble at Opie and did a peace sign. She did one back.

Mulaki and Xu sat cross-legged with Troy and Bear. Opie joined them and they sat in a circle.

Opie suddenly understood. "Is this group therapy?"

"No," Xu said. "A gang of secret superheroes. I did say." He ran his hand through his hair, posing.

Opie watched him fuss with his fringe. "Right. And we're going to stop an evil billionaire from turning my school into a warehouse?"

"Oh, Varling wants to do much more than that," Xu said.

Xu glanced around and leaned into the circle. Everyone copied him. It was the classic 'I'm-about-to-tell-you-a-secret' move, and you *always* want to hear what comes next.

"Varling is targeting your school. He has a team of mind readers who stand at the edge of your playground every break time, get in the students' heads and wind them up until they fight each other."

"I KNEW something was going on!" Opie gasped. Her horror was mixed with pride that her suspicions were right.

"He thinks children should leave school at eleven years old," said Xu. "He reckons it's a waste of time educating children when they could be working in his factories."

"He thinks your small hands are perfect for packing things into boxes," said Bear, nodding at Opie's hands.

Opie examined them. They were small and she *was* good at wrapping birthday presents.

"So," said Mulaki, "he keeps giving newspaper interviews and television interviews where he says schools are full of kids fighting and misbehaving. 'Hotbeds of trouble,' he calls them. He has been using Saint Francis of Assisi as an example. I think about half of your whole school are excluded for fighting now. We think he's going to take a camera crew to your school and show everyone what a waste of tax money it is. Or something worse. We don't know his exact plan yet."

"But . . . but . . ." Opie was outraged. "Kids always go to school!"

"In lots of place round the world they don't," said Bear. "They go to work when they're your age to support their families. Varling thinks that's a great idea."

"For all kids?" Opie said.

"No, he wouldn't do it to rich people or his friends' kids," said Bear.

Opie looked around the circle. "Are there more people coming?"

"No, just us four."

"Are you a bit –"

"Understaffed? Yes," Bear admitted.

"There *were* thirty of us," Mulaki said. "But they've been poached one by one by Varling."

"Because they didn't realise there are some things more important than money," said Xu fiercely.

"Said the rich kid," Troy muttered and Bear snorted.

"Batman was a rich kid!" Xu retorted. "I'm basically Batman."

Mulaki rolled her eyes, clearly this was an old argument.

"I have a question." Opie raised her hand out of school habit. "Why do you meet in a field?"

"It's very noisy being a mind reader. Don't you find it's quieter away from people?" said Troy.

"But I can still hear them?" said Opie.

Troy and Bear looked impressed.

"You can?" Xu asked.

"Yeah." The voices had been chatting away at the edges of her mind.

"Who are you hearing?" Mulaki asked.

Opie shrugged helplessly.

"Look for clues," Bear told her. "How many are there?"

Opie thought. There were so many voices, and they were so small, it was like brushing her fingers across grains of sand. "Thousands," she said. "Tens of thousands."

She was rewarded with a circle of deeply impressed faces. Troy stood up and looked out over the long grass. Bear got up and stood with him, jumping to see further.

"That's the city centre," Troy said, pointing across

the park to a cluster of tall buildings.

"That's miiiiiles away," marvelled Bear.

They both turned and stared at Opie. She tucked her fringe behind her ear, feeling unusually confident.

Mulaki gave Opie her full attention. When Mulaki wasn't terrifying Opie, she was like a cool teacher. That was the highest compliment Opie could give any adult.

"Opie, I think you're a very powerful mind reader. I think it's time to test you and see what you can do, okay?"

"Definitely," said Opie, excited. She liked exams and this felt like a magical exam. She couldn't wait to start being a superhero and reading people's minds.

"Well," said Troy, reading *her* mind. "You don't always want to know what people are thinking. I had a, um, brave haircut last year and all I could hear was 'Oof, that's brutal, he looks like a trophy with those ears'."

"I don't remember that haircut," said Bear.

"I bought a hat immediately."

"I remember when you wore a hat a lot."

"So that was that."

"Well *I* heard literally all my Christmas presents in advance," pouted Xu. "The stupid butler."

"I hear death," said Opie and everyone stopped laughing at Xu. "Death and fear every night."

"Where do you *live*?" Troy asked.

"It's quite a rough area," whispered Xu.

"It's really not!" protested Opie.

"Well, we'll get to the bottom of it," said Xu darkly. "Don't worry, Opie, you're protected by . . ." He made a shape with his fingers and whispered, *"The Resistance."*

There was a silence. Opie narrowed her eyes. "Sorry, what was –?"

"He's trying to give us a catchphrase," said Bear. "Make us more official, so we're not just . . ."

"Sitting in a field hiding from the voices in your head," Opie said tactlessly.

"Well, we look even weirder now we've got a ten-year-old, so take some responsibility for that," Xu sniped.

"We might be weirdos sitting in a field," said Mulaki. "But we're going to teach you to push those voices aside and only hear them when you want to."

"I never want to," said Opie fervently.

"We need you to when you're trained and a member of The Resistance," said Xu.

Which was bossy, as Opie had never actually said she wanted to join. But obviously she wanted to join. A secret organisation of mind readers? Yes please. This was so cool. Even if Bear was old and Xu dressed weirdly.

Opie peeked out at everyone from beneath her fringe.

"Yes mate," said Bear drily. "We all heard that."

Yeah I get people sitting on my molehill. Seen a lot of bums perched on the top of this tunnel. It's a posh area, so mainly red trousers.

Never had someone land head first in it though. That was a first. Gave me the shock of my life.

CHAPTER ELEVEN

IN THE HEART OF **LONDON**, WHERE ALL THE BUILDINGS are made of glass and touch the sky, a man sat in his office at the top of the tallest skyscraper.

It had the name VARLING emblazoned on the side in golden letters because it was owned by Hugo Varling. He was a very rich man who owned four houses, a plane and a private island and *still* needed to put his name on things to feel special. He had blond hair, a tiny nose and bright blue eyes, and looked like he had been fed on the most expensive food his whole life.

Max Inkelaar sat opposite Hugo, one long leg slung over his knee. He was lean and craggy and looked like he had lived a harder life than his boss.

The two men were feeling very smug.

"So nearly half the children at Saint Francis of Assisi are now excluded or expelled," Hugo said. "How long to get the other half gone?"

"I anticipate the teachers will start separating them into smaller groups at recreational break times, minimising the opportunities for them to be alone."

Hugo hated the way Max spoke: all long words, said slowly.

Max smiled. He knew he was annoying Hugo. He was doing it on purpose. When you have a horrible boss, you do what you can to get your own back. He was a mind reader but Hugo was not.

"And what about that other lot, are they still meeting in a park?"

"Yes, they have a new recruit."

"Oh?" Hugo looked wary.

"A child."

Hugo shivered dramatically. "I'm fwightened."

The two men laughed. But Hugo's mood changed suddenly. He was like that.

"Still," he brooded, instantly moody. "I want them on our team. We bought all the others. We can buy them."

"Hugo, it's four mind readers. They meet in a park."

"Five, now. Isn't it?"

"Four and a half. We have twenty-five adults."

"I want them all!" Hugo shouted, like a big baby having a tantrum.

"They're not Pokémon," Max muttered, as close to rudeness as he dared.

Hugo bounced his fountain pen on the desk in a rapid, irritable rat-a-tat-tat. "Who are we trying to poach now?"

"Troy. He's not moving."

Hugo snorted. "Just wait till his nieces are working in my warehouses. He'll want money then."

I really really don't like you, Max thought, looking at his boss. "We'll have the school empty by October and they'll have to shut it down," he reassured Hugo out loud.

"October?" Hugo pouted. "I want the school NOW. I want to build that warehouse ASAP, fill it with products and get kids working. They're so small and quick; they'll work twice as hard as adults too because they're scared of being shouted at."

"I don't think we can."

"I don't like to hear no," said Hugo.

Ugh, thought Max. I bet he saw that on a film and thought it sounded tough. "Well," he said, "why don't we stage something big? Some school trip where they can run amok in public? We'll grab photos and get them all expelled in one go."

"Yes! Do that! They'd all be expelled and Saint Francis of Assisi would be mine!" Hugo spun in his chair, looking like all his Christmases had come at once. "I love getting what I want," he said dreamily.

"I've noticed," said Max. He scratched the stubble on his chin.

Hugo stared at Max for a long moment. "You feeling bad for the poor kiddies, Max?"

Max shrugged, not wanting to be honest with his boss and say, "Yes, this feels like a horrible thing to do to hundreds of kids."

"See this vase?" Hugo pointed at a massive decorative vase. "This is where I keep all the damns I give about kids." He grabbed the vase, tipped it upside down and started shaking it furiously. Nothing fell out.

"It's empty, Max!" he cried. "It's empty cos I don't give a damn about kids!"

Hugo thought he was very funny, but he wasn't a laughing sort of person. So he said, "That's really funny!"

Max got up and left his stupid man-baby boss shaking a priceless vase. Every time Max met with Hugo he felt morally unclean, like he needed a long scrub in the shower.

When you're looking for a place to build your chrysalis, it's location, location, location.

I'm only in there for twenty days but once I'm in, I'm in! I can't crawl out, half caterpillar/half butterfly and drag my bum across town.

And you don't want to emerge, unfurl your majestic wings in the middle of a market and now you smell of fried onions.

CHAPTER TWELVE

THE RESISTANCE HAD BEEN SITTING IN THE PARK FOR hours. Opie had not managed to read a single mind and noses were beginning to burn in the sun. Troy was making a daisy chain to avoid looking at Opie and embarrassing her. (The daisy chain had grown really long.) The four superheroes were not impressed and Opie's dream of joining The Resistance seemed impossible. She felt panicky and a little hopeless.

"Take a break, Opie," said Mulaki.

Opie hated giving up but she was exhausted with concentrating so hard. She flopped back on the warm crunchy grass.

"No one's an expert at first," said Troy. "When I was ten, I had no idea I even was a mind reader. I kept answering questions people were thinking, not saying. It freaked my whole family out."

"But you can all read minds easily now, right?" Opie asked.

"Oh yeah. And not only that, we can push emotions and thoughts into peoples' minds. Big crowds of people," Troy told her.

"Mind control?" Opie was shocked.

"We don't do it for fun!" Bear assured her.

"Yeah, we have ethics," Xu sighed. "Mulaki makes us have them."

"We mainly use our powers to stop Varling. He'll put mind readers outside your school every day, making pupils fight until they've all been excluded and you're the only one left. They won't get in your head, though, once you get the hang of your powers." The Resistance leader smiled kindly.

"*If* you have powers," Xu muttered quietly.

Opie got goosebumps, remembering the first time Mulaki told her she was special. For a moment today, she had started to believe it. She hoped Mulaki was right and she hadn't made a mistake. Opie enjoyed feeling special. It was a new experience.

"Maybe we'll give up for today?" said Troy. "I've got work soon."

They started wading back to the car through the long grass. Mulaki squeezed Opie's shoulder and Bear ruffled her hair. They knew she felt bad.

A few hours ago, Opie was a member of a gang. For a whole afternoon, she wasn't tagging along behind Jackson and Cillian; she had her own gang, and a superhero skill! *Opie Jones: Mind Reader.* She loved the way that sounded. She wanted to write it all over her schoolbooks.

But she didn't feel special any more.

Opie could feel those other voices still chatting at

the edge of her mind. They'd fallen silent while she'd been with The Resistance and concentrating hard, but she was tired now. The voices took advantage of that, and scuttled in.

If they weren't The Resistance's thoughts, or the thoughts of people in the city, what *were* they?

Opie sank to her knees by a big flat rock. The chatter got louder. It sounded like hundreds of voices all

pushing past each other, squirming into her mind.

"Opie? Are you okay?" Bear tried to look at her face.

"Has she caught the sun?" Mulaki asked, concerned.

The Resistance crowded around Opie but she ignored them, putting her hands on the rock, determined to lift it. Troy bent to help her, and they finally flipped it over. The voices in her head were suddenly loud and clear.

Opie looked down.

Thousands of insects were crawling over each other, scuttling over the back of the rock and on the ground, twisting through mud. Their thoughts were filling Opie's head as clearly as if they were talking.

Opie recoiled, her hands over her ears, though of course that didn't help. Xu opened his mouth. Opie couldn't hear him but she knew he was laughing.

I do know where I'm going thank you, Hilary, and we would get there a lot quicker without you second-guessing me. Please would you hurry up at the back, Hannah. I have an itinerary and it should come as no surprise to any of you lolly-gaggers that your collective inability to find your shoes before we leave the house has thrown all of my timings out of whack. So thank you for that.

Come ON, Hannah!

CHAPTER THIRTEEN

OPIE SAT IN THE PASSENGER SEAT OF **MULAKI'S CAR,** arms folded, fringe over her face. An *insect* mind-reader. This was weak tea.

Opie sighed. She'd be home soon and she'd have to tell her parents she didn't get into that fake summer school for kids who liked books more than sunshine. And she was going to spend the rest of her life listening to earwigs argue.

Mulaki glanced at her. "Don't feel bad, kid. It's amazing to be able to read insect minds. Did you know, there's more insects in the world than people?"

"There are over two hundred million insects for every human being," said Opie, who had a good memory for facts. No one appreciated this until they were playing a quiz.

"You're very smart," said Mulaki.

This was usually Opie's favourite thing to hear but now all she wanted to hear was, 'You're in The Resistance, kid!'

But Mulaki did not say that. Instead she said, trying to be nice; "I wish *I* knew what insects thought."

"It's a lot of e*at mud eat mud eat mud,* to be honest."

"Oh right. I can imagine."

Mulaki put some music on the radio and wound down the windows, letting the warm evening air in. As they drove away from the park and back to the city, Opie nodded along to the music, feeling cheerier. Maybe she'd get an insect sidekick. Something big enough to have a face. Nothing that scuttled or oozed, Jackson would get grossed out.

Opie took her phone out and googled *stag beetle.*

They drove on in silence. Opie started thinking that if she was never going to see Mulaki again, she should ask all the questions she could now.

"Um, how many people can you mind control at once?"

Mulaki was stern. "I don't say mind control, Opie.

It's sinister to make people do what you want."

"Okay, but . . ."

"But a really powerful mind reader could walk down the road and cause a riot behind them. Or, by the time they looked back, hundreds of people would be singing, dancing and hugging."

"Are you a really powerful mind reader?" Opie asked.

"I'm the most powerful one I know, these days."

Opie wanted to ask who Mulaki had known before who was more powerful than her. But Mulaki's face looked sad and Opie stayed silent. Mulaki kept talking, her eyes on the road.

"I spend most of my time trying to drive bad thoughts out of people's heads after Varling's lot have made them angry. That is really fiddly work. It's the difference between playing tennis against someone, and knocking a ball against a wall. The wall isn't trying to beat you."

Mulaki glanced across at Opie. "You're still a sort of mind reader though," she said. "So you can teach yourself to put a shield around your mind, stop Varling's team from reading your thoughts. That might be useful."

"Yes, I ... I guess," said Opie, trying to feel enthusiastic about this 'superskill'. BLANK GIRL, she could call herself. QUIET HEAD. THE VOID. That would be like school where no one bothered to talk to her because apparently she was shy. She didn't fancy that.

They were nearly at Opie's home. And she was panicking that she'd never see Mulaki again so she tried another way of staying in touch.

"I know I can't help you with your Resistance work," she said. "But are you on social media? I could build you a website, run your Twitter account. My mum does it for my dad."

"Thanks Opie," said Mulaki kindly. "But I'm not sure a secret underground superhero rebellion should have a website."

"Oh . . . yeah."

They were on Opie's street. She could already see her block of flats. So she asked one last question she'd been wondering about.

"Mulaki? Do you ever play poker and use your mind-reading skills to win?"

"No! Never," said Mulaki firmly.

They pulled up outside Opie's block of flats.

"You wouldn't do that because you're a good boy," Opie said dreamily.

"Because I – what?" Mulaki turned to look at her passenger. "Are you okay? You have a funny look on your face."

Opie wiped some dribble off her chin. "Sorry," she said. "I just – I thought you said you were a good boy."

"Why would I say that?"

"I don't know."

Mulaki put her hand on Opie's forehead. "Go in and have some water. You caught a lot of sun today."

"Thanks. Um. Bye forever then," said Opie sadly, and stumbled out of the car.

"Bye Opie," Mulaki said kindly. "You're still special. You're an insect mind-reader!"

"Yeah, thanks, cool, cheers," said Opie, giving a brave little thumbs up and heading to her front door, past a black and white dog sitting patiently outside.

I am a good boy.

Ways in which I am a good boy include:

1. Sitting.

2. Not freaking out when I see next door's cat.

3. Eating toast very gently from your hand even though I am excited by the toast.

5. When you accidentally throw a stick I will bring it back to you and if you throw it again I will go and get it for you again because everyone makes mistakes sometimes.

CHAPTER FOURTEEN

OPIE CLOSED THE FRONT DOOR, LEANED AGAINST IT AND fought the urge to scream with excitement. She felt her cheeks. They were bright red and she couldn't stop smiling.

She'd read that dog's mind. She'd definitely read his mind!

She wasn't an insect mind-reader. She was an *animal* mind-reader.

Mulaki had driven off before Opie'd had a chance to tell her. She didn't know how to get hold of her now. Surely an animal mind-reader could join The Resistance?

That was all Opie wanted now. To join The Resistance, to save her school and also, let's be honest, be part of a cool gang of superheroes. Jackson would definitely want to be best friends then.

Opie smiled, enjoying a very petty daydream where Cillian finally invited her to his birthday party and she couldn't go because she was working with The Resistance and he spent his whole birthday listening to Jackson wondering what Opie was up to.

"How was the special school for kids who prefer kids to books?" Harvey called from the living room. His memory was back to normal.

"It . . . was fine," Opie said slowly. She wasn't used to lying to her parents and was not very good at it. "They said I was very clever."

"Well, duh, yeah you are," said Harvey comfortably.

"Opie, are you all right? You're talking like a robot," Violet said, concerned.

"I'll . . . get a glass of water," Opie said and scurried into the kitchen.

"Can I have an ice lolly while you're there?" Harvey called.

"Dad! You are living off ice lollies. You'll have a stick running through you soon."

Harvey made a joke about it poking out of his bum, which no one needed or enjoyed.

Opie took her parents an ice lolly each and headed to bed, exhausted from her strange day. It was only early evening, so she lay on top of her covers, fully dressed and reading a book. As it got darker outside, she had to flick on her bedside reading light to see her book – and she started to hear familiar voices.

Where aaaaare yooooooou
I'm coming to get yoooooo.
Come out to play . . . I'm hungry.

But this time, rather than shivering with fear, Opie sat up in bed, thinking.

She jumped out of bed, hurried lightly downstairs, past her parents watching TV and sneaked out of the back door.

Opie stood outside the block of flats with a huge smile on her face and stared up into the oak trees behind them. There was silence. Then something up there shifted its weight, causing the leaves to rustle.

Opie clapped her hands and said one word aloud to herself.

"Owls."

Above her head, a branch trembled as an owl launched itself into the air. She heard familiar panicking thoughts down by her feet.

The owls were hunting.

Opie turned on her heel and raced to the kitchen, where she sifted through the recycling bin at top speed until she found everything she needed. After a bit of hasty cutting and sticking at the kitchen counter, she headed back out, cradling a pile of plastic.

"Everything all right?" Harvey asked, but Opie was already outside again.

On her hands and knees on the grass, Opie gently filled an empty biscuit box with stones, making it heavy. Then she half-buried the small plastic triangle from inside a chocolate box, leaving a tiny gap at the top. She scrabbled at it, making claw hands like an owl, pleased to find she couldn't lift it.

Opie stood back and examined her work. She had studded the ground outside the flat with tiny hiding places made of plastic containers from the kitchen bin.

The sun had set but the ground and buildings still hummed with heat. Opie was *really* ready for bed now. She hoped her efforts out here would give her a good night's sleep for once.

Back upstairs, Opie stood by her window. She

hadn't dared to open them for days, but now she would. The glass still felt warm to her touch as she opened the windows wide. The fresh air poured into her bedroom, bringing in a honeysuckle smell.

Almost immediately the voices began, clearer than ever. They weren't as scary now she knew she was hearing mice. Mice who would hopefully be saved from a sudden, crunchy death.

Run run run hide scared tired keep running can't keep running. Scared scared scar– OOOO!

A mouse, fleeing for its life, had found one of the hiding places and escaped an owl's clutches.

Hehehe. Hiding.

The little voice in her head sounded smug.

Hehehe.
Safe.
Shush.

Fury filled Opie's mind as an owl rose into the air, beating big silent wings. He'd lost his meal.

Opie smiled blissfully, and closed her eyes. If she concentrated hard, she could actually *see* what the mouse was seeing: the inside of an empty Jaffa Cake box, the bottom covered in stones. The mouse picked one up and turned it over, huge in his little paws, still warm from the sun.

There was a scrabbling noise as the owl landed and made a second attempt. It tried to grab hold of the box with its claws and tip the mouse out. But Opie had thought of that. The stones made it too heavy and the plastic was too smooth to get a grip.

Opie's eyes opened again. She listened to the rasping voice in her head complaining bitterly about the unfairness of life.

She took three bowls of nuts and crisps outside, as a consolation prize for the hunters, hoping they were a good substitute for mice. In the tree an owl sat and sulked, preening his feathers while Opie laid out a picnic on the grass for him.

Three floors up, one of her neighbours opened his

window and stared out at what Opie was up to. "Oh. Kaaay," he said, in the flat tone of a man who had work in the morning and didn't have time for this. He shut the window and turned off his light.

Like, I'm not being funny or nothing. But I thought we had a good relationship. He's got his allotment to take care of, I've got all the mud-eating ... I'm very into that.

We don't chat much but I thought we were cordial.

Then one day, out of the blue, he wallops his spade down on me! Cuts me in two!

I'm literally like an inch shorter and, not being funny, but I need that inch for work. My wife said it was nothing personal. I said it may be nothing personal, Harriet, but it certainly wasn't polite!

I feel very let down by him actually. Soon as I find my inch, Harriet and me, we're off and looking for a less violent place to work.

CHAPTER FIFTEEN

OPIE SIGHED. SHE COULD STILL HEAR THAT WORM whingeing about the Decline of Good Manners. He was unbearably dull. Was this life as an animal mind reader? She must be literally the least exciting superhero in the world.

Opie was spending Sunday on the grass outside the flat, practising isolating her own thoughts from the animal ones that popped into her head. She needed a human mind reader to practise on, but didn't want The Resistance to know her plan until she'd perfected it. Opie hated failing at things.

She had been thinking . . . The animal mind-reading was cool but she didn't know how The Resistance would feel about it. She had a nasty feeling that Xu would still find it funny and hardly a promotion from insects.

BUT Mulaki had definitely said that if Varling's men couldn't read Opie's mind, that would be useful to The Resistance. So that's what Opie was going to do. If the only way into the gang was to be BLANK GIRL, CAPTAIN VOID HEAD, then that is what Opie would do.

She was practising by pushing animal thoughts out of her head. Above her was a tree full of little birds thinking panicky thoughts and never once finishing a sentence. Underneath her, worms were complaining, drearily and pedantically. And she was concentrating on pushing them all out of her head until it was blissfully quiet.

She was getting there. Bit by bit. She imagined inflating a balloon in her head, then blowing it up slowly and pushing everything out of her brain. It was very relaxing.

In the distance Opie could hear boys whooping. The whooping got louder and she peeked out from beneath her fringe to see that it was Jackson. With Cillian, of course.

Jackson and Cillian cycled towards her on brand new bikes.

"Wanna watch us do stunts?" Jackson asked, bouncing on his back wheel.

It was more interesting than the worm, so Opie said, "Sure!"

Jackson and Cillian bounced on their back wheels, whooping encouragingly at each other. Opie waited for them to start doing their stunts. They looked expectantly at her.

"Oh," she said. "This is it?"

Cillian stopped bouncing and dropped one foot to the floor. He was scathing. "I'm sorry, could you do it, Dopey?"

"Probably yes, with like ten minutes' practice," Opie said.

"Wow. Rude. So rude."

Cillian was ready to leave, but Jackson wasn't offended. He stopped bouncing too.

"It *feels* impressive when you're doing it!" he panted. "What are you doing anyway?"

"Hanging out with her friends. Can't you see?" said Cillian, gesturing at the empty patch of grass.

"Um, actually," said Opie, delighted that, for once, she got to surprise Cillian by being cool and interesting. She tucked her fringe behind her ears and told them everything. The voices at night, her ability to read animal minds, The Resistance (she showed them the Resistance symbol) and Varling's plans to empty their school and buy it and how The Resistance wanted her help except, um, well . . . she wasn't sure if they wanted her any more because they thought she could only read insect minds, but in fact she could read all animals' minds, which was probably more useful? And she was discovering she had some pretty sweet skills, including the ability to keep mind readers out of her head.

"And, and . . no, that's it, that's everything," she said, dry-mouthed after talking at them for five solid minutes.

"Wow!" Jackson breathed, gazing at Opie like she was magic.

Cillian hated this. "That sounds great, Dopey, and not at all completely made up!" he breathed in a similar voice to Jackson.

"I'll prove it," Opie shrugged, feeling bold.

"What's that ladybird thinking?" Cillian demanded, pointing at a ladybird.

Opie hesitated. "That's actually a bad example because she's asleep."

The three of them bent down and stared at the ladybird who was sitting very still on a sunny leaf.

"That's convenient," Cillian said sweetly.

Even Jackson looked doubtful. "It's a cool story,

Opie," he said kindly. "It's still a skill to tell good stories."

"No, wait," Opie said, getting flustered. She leaned closer towards the ladybird.

OPIE
Excuse me. Um. Excuse me?

Cillian yawned. "Sorry," he said when Opie looked

around. "Was I harshing your psychic vibes?"

Irritated, Opie turned back to the ladybird.

OPIE

Oi!

LADYBIRD

Ah! Ah! Ah! Ah!

The ladybird opened her wings and fluttered about in a panic.

OPIE

Sorry sorry sorry! I just wanted to talk.

LADYBIRD

I was SLEEPING!

OPIE

Sorry!

LADYBIRD

I don't care if you're sorry. Don't go around shouting at folks while they're asleep and then you won't have anything to apologise for!

OPIE
Yeah, no, that's a really good point, sorry.

The ladybird flew away, fluttering her wings with tiny fury.

LADYBIRD
... Flipping maniac.

Opie turned to Cillian and Jackson.

"What did she say?" Jackson asked.

"She . . . said she was sleeping . . ." Opie said.

"Well, sure, that makes sense," said Jackson.

"That's me one hundred per cent convinced," said Cillian. "But for a bonus point. What's that dog thinking?" He pointed at a dog with its head hanging out of a car window. The car was travelling fast on a road twenty feet from the three of them.

Opie felt helpless. "That dog's too far away and travelling too fast!"

"Probably thinking WEEEEEEEEEE!! Isn't he,

Opie?" said Jackson, trying to help but making her sound bonkers.

Opie nodded. "I mean, yeah? Very probably."

"Oh! I know an animal you can talk to!" Jackson said. "My aunt has a budgie! Let's go now, she won't mind!"

Jackson grabbed Opie by the hand and pulled her to her feet. They headed off, wheeling his bike. Cillian was forced to follow behind, furious.

Jackson was full of ideas for what they could do with Opie's new skill. "We must turn this into a business! I'd be your manager, you're the 'talent' . . ."

"What am I?" Cillian grouched, hurrying to catch up.

"Security. Or publicity, whatever," said Jackson over his shoulder in an offhand tone which Cillian hated and Opie loved.

I love my brother, he so pretty.
  Look, imma tap his face.
  With my beak. He doesn't mind.
  I tap him again.
  He so pretty.
  Tap
            Tap
                        Tap.

CHAPTER SIXTEEN

OPIE'S GOOD MOOD LASTED RIGHT UP UNTIL SHE MET her first customer.

OPIE
That's a mirror.

Opie told the budgie for the third time, slumped with her head in her hands.

OPIE
You're looking in a mirror. It's your reflection.

BUDGIE
Is it now?

The budgie examined his reflection and seemed like he was taking on board what Opie was saying.

BUDGIE
That is super interesting, lady.

"Are you two getting on well?"

Jackson's Aunt Connie had opened her front door to find Jackson, Cillian and Opie on the doorstep, with Jackson announcing that Opie was "a *professional* animal mind-reader!"

"Amazing, come in!" she'd said.

"Professional means she gets paid," Jackson informed his aunt as he walked past.

"Sorry," Opie whispered. "I really don't need to be paid."

Now the budgie tapped the mirror with his beak, making his reflection wobble.

BUDGIE

What do you think, bruv? Do we like refrexions?

Opie had never wanted to punch a budgie before. This feathery wally was a first. All she needed was him to tell her something only he would know . . . embarrassing TV shows Connie liked, or the pet name she called him; anything to convince Jackson and Cillian that she could read his mind.

But he wasn't answering her simplest questions.

"Is he happy?" Aunt Connie asked.

Opie thought the bird was such a dum-dum he'd be happy if he was on fire. 'I'm super-warm!' he'd announce cheerfully.

"Maybe he could do with a friend?" Opie suggested.

"Of course!" Connie made a note on her phone.

"Although," Opie said, "he's convinced his reflection is his brother. So if you got him another bird, he'd think there were four of them in there, and might feel overcrowded?"

Jackson, Cillian, Connie and Opie stared thoughtfully

at the budgie. He stared back. Aunt Connie deleted
the note on her phone.

"Peep!" the budgie chirped at them.

"Ooh, Opie, what's he saying?" Jackson was
excited

"Peep. He's literally saying and thinking . . . 'peep'."

Opie ignored Cillian's smirking face and focused

on Aunt Connie. "He is happy," she assured Jackson's aunt. "He loves the seeds you give him. He thinks the view from his cage is 'mad wicked'. He's very enthusiastic about his water."

"Seriously?" Connie gasped, like Opie was revealing something fascinating. "It's just tap water."

"He loves it."

"I shouldn't treat him to some bottled water or . . .?"

"No no, tap is fine."

They ran out of things to say at this point.

"Love a bit of tap water, me," said Aunt Connie.

"Peep!"

"And that's just 'peep' again," Opie translated.

There was a squealing noise from the street outside as a car raced past the house.

"Maniacs!" Aunt Connie tutted.

But Opie's eyes lit up as she caught a glimpse of the car: a distinctive pearl-coloured old sports car with black details. Opie had only seen one of those cars before. She was certain Mulaki and Xu had just driven past them at top speed.

"The Resistance," she mouthed at Jackson, who

immediately leaped into action.

"Aunt Connie, we must go," he said importantly.

"Must we?" grumped Cillian, who was halfway through a biscuit and a cup of tea.

"Wait, must we?" said Opie, alarmed.

"Yes!" said Jackson, and did The Resistance mime at her. Opie was impressed by how well he'd remembered it. Monsieur Lunarca underestimated him.

Cillian looked sour and Opie *knew* he was trying to think of a rude word that rhymed with Resistance. It would end in 'pants'.

Jackson hustled his friends out of the door.

"Thank you for having us!" Opie called over her shoulder to Jackson's aunt, remembering her manners.

She hurried after Cillian as he manoeuvred his bike down the stairwell out of Connie's flat. Then she glanced back to see Jackson holding his bike up with one hand and stuffing five-pound notes into his pocket with the other.

"Wait, what are we doing, Jackson?" Opie asked.

"There's obviously an emergency," said Jackson. "The Resistance are responding and they'll need your help. Like, Avengers Assemble, right?"

"Only if there's, like, a dog or a pig in trouble. And then, what can she do except read its mind and say 'Yeah, it's pretty stressed right now'?" said Cillian drily.

Opie HATED it when she agreed with Cillian. But Jackson was adamant. He helped Opie stand behind him on his bike, one foot balanced on each side of the back wheel and her hands on his shoulders. This was the coolest Opie had ever felt or looked. She hoped that someone from school would see her and spread the word.

"Can you hear them? Like, um, telepathically?" Jackson called over his shoulder as they cycled down the road in the direction of Mulaki's car.

"Aahhh . . ." Opie furiously hunted through the constant chatter in her mind for any clues, but it was difficult. She felt light-headed and her left foot slipped a little on Jackson's wheel hub.

"Careful!" He grabbed her leg and held on until she adjusted her foot and was secure again.

"Which way, Dopey?" Cillian skidded to a halt as the road reached a T-junction.

Opie scowled. She wished he wasn't here. She didn't KNOW which way. She ran a hand over the back of her neck. This was not the weather for stress. Her hair was so thick, it was making her hot.

MARGOT
YOUR hair's thick? Nice one. Look at ME.

Margot was stomping down the pavement with a face like thunder and (Opie didn't want to mention it) a leaf stuck to her bum.

OPIE
Have you seen a sports car going really fast?

MARGOT
Yeah.

Margot kept walking past them. Opie fought the urge to be snide.

OPIE
Could you please tell me more about it?

MARGOT
Parked up down Station Road.

OPIE
Thank you!

MARGOT
Whev.

Opie turned to Jackson and Cillian, who were watching this silent interaction with interest (Jackson) and disbelief (Cillian).

"Station Road!" she announced.

"Did the cat tell you that?" said Cillian, speaking gently as if to a toddler.

"Yes, Cill-i-an." Opie met sarcasm with sarcasm. "She did."

I'm in!

Moving house is such a faff but think I've got everything done.

So yeah, feeling pretty optimistic. I hope I'll come out a beautiful butterfly but then looks aren't everything, are they?

It'll be great to be able to fly. I can go see my cousins across town.

But for now just gonna chillax, enjoy the peace and quiet for twenty days.

CHAPTER SEVENTEEN

OPIE HELD ON TIGHTLY TO JACKSON'S SHOULDERS AS he cycled down the road towards the station, with Cillian in hot pursuit.

As they got closer, Opie spotted Mulaki's parked sports car. Mulaki and Xu were clambering out and hurrying across the road, picking their way through people and cars. There were adults talking in groups and looking serious. Opie, Jackson and Cillian pulled up and looked around. Something serious was going on.

A police car drove up behind them and hooted its horn gently. Opie hopped off Jackson's back wheel as Jackson and Cillian quickly waddled their bikes out of the way and let the car through.

Opie spotted Mulaki glancing back and lifted her

hand in an awkward half wave. Mulaki said something to Xu, who hurried over to the three of them.

"Xu, these are my friends, Jackson and Cillian," Opie said. Cillian stared at Xu's velvet culottes but said nothing, even about being called Opie's 'friend'. The serious atmosphere was making all three of them quiet.

Xu nodded briefly at the boys. "Is there a football team at your school? Training on a Sunday?"

"Um, I think so?" Opie was baffled by the odd question.

"Yes," Cillian piped up. "My cousin plays. Why?"

"Did you see them on the news? They were spotted running out of the playing field. Their coach said they just turned and ran, charged down the High Street smashing up shop fronts and car windows, and now they've gone missing. One of them has his little sister with him."

"Why would they smash shop windows?" Cillian wondered.

Xu and Opie exchanged a look. "Varling's mind readers," Opie guessed and Xu nodded. Opie had a nasty memory of what Lottie had said about Evelyn, how her face went blank as she ran into a group of people. Varling's telepaths could make a person lose all self-control.

"They'll all be expelled, I imagine. Varling will love that, ten kids gone in one day," Xu said grimly. "But right now we're just trying to find them. They're not in their right minds. They could get into real danger."

"I thought Varling just wanted them expelled, not hurt?"

"He doesn't care, Opie." Xu turned back to the search party. "Want to help us?"

"Yes!" Opie hurried after Xu, with Cillian and Jackson trailing behind her, unusually shy – but then, Xu wasn't like any other adults they'd met. "By the way, Xu, I can read animal minds, not just insects!"

Xu looked unexcited. "Good for you, I guess?"

Opie refused to meet Cillian's eye.

"Come on." Xu grabbed her hand. "We need to move quickly. The football team were running, they could be anywhere by now. You know how to skim-read a book?"

"Yes!" Opie felt on safer ground. This was something she did at school. "You run your finger down the middle of a page of words and glance at all the words as you go down, like out of the corners of your eyes, so you don't read every word but you grab enough of them to understand what's happening."

"Right." Xu was amused by her wordy answer. "Well, that's how I search human minds, so maybe you can do it with animal ones? Here." He handed Opie his phone. There was a photo of a serious-faced toddler in a princess dress and frog wellies. "That's the little sister, Olive. She's only five."

Xu strode across the road. His long legs covered the ground easily and Opie had to sprint to keep up. She tried her best to concentrate. She was desperate to prove to Xu that she belonged in The Resistance. She was running, reading animal minds AND trying to keep the image of Olive in the front of her mind.

Xu stopped suddenly and she bumped into the back of him.

"No no, that's not her," he muttered.

He started running again, face pointed upwards like

a bloodhound trying to smell something on the breeze. No one looked very smart when they were mind-reading.

Four motorbikes raced past them with a screaming roar of engines, making them both jump. Xu gripped Opie's hand so tightly it hurt. They crunched through a pile of broken glass. Opie wondered if the football club had done that. She glanced back, Jackson and Cillian were following but at a slight distance. She hadn't seen either of them look so nervous before. She gave them a thumbs up but it reassured no one, not even her.

Xu darted left and right, raced towards something but then stopped dead. Opie clung on, feeling like useless dead weight. Any minute he'd leave her behind. She wasn't reading any minds. She was too flustered, she couldn't think straight.

Xu pivoted again, and Opie tripped and fell flat on her face. She lay there a second, winded.

"I'm sorry," said Xu, bending to help her up. "I just – what?"

"Shush." Opie held a hand up and stayed where

she'd fallen, face down on the grass verge. She felt vibrations in the ground as Cillian and Jackson ran up to join Xu.

"Why's Dopey snogging mud?" Cillian said.

"Shut UP!" Opie hissed.

She could hear something beneath her.

Not being funny right but at the end of the day I can get along with most people, I am a people person. And I wasn't bothering him, I'd just never seen a frog that big before.

I wanted a quick chat, pleasantries, but he wouldn't answer me. Just kept smiling. I'm not judging or anything but that is weird.

Opie pressed her ear harder into the soft ground. That was a worm, she was sure of it. She'd know that dreary tone anywhere.

"Opie, we have to go . . ." Xu was trying to pick her up but she gestured firmly at him to stop.

The worm was talking about a big grinning frog that didn't talk back. Opie remembered the image of Olive:

a serious sturdy child in a princess dress and frog wellies.

OPIE
Hello. Do you know where the frog went?

WORM
Oh hello. Can't say for definite I'm afraid.

OPIE
It is important.

WORM
Okay, let me think . . . I heard crunching?

OPIE
Crisps?

WORM
Gravel. I am somewhat of an expert in soil and things of that nature. My wife, Audrey –

AUDREY

Hello.

OPIE

Hello.

WORM

– specialises in compost, for example –

AUDREY

Oh love, I wouldn't hold myself up as a specialist –

OPIE

Gotta go, thank you!

Opie lifted herself on to her hands and knees and looked around for gravel. Past Jackson, Cillian and Xu's feet, she spotted a gravel path, sloping down and out of sight.

She jumped up, pushed past Xu and sprinted towards the path. It was heading straight for the railway line. There was a tall metal fence at the bottom that prevented people from stumbling into the path of trains but . . .

She reached the fence and skidded to a halt. There was a missing bar at the bottom, small enough for a toddler to squeeze through, but too small for Opie. She ran along the fence, trying to find a way in. When she found a hole, she started to crawl through, feeling the wire snagging her T-shirt.

"Hang on," said Jackson, who had followed her with Xu and Cillian. "Ah ah ow . . ."

He held back the wire with Xu's help, making the hole big enough for Opie. Once Jackson and Xu had followed Opie through the hole in the fence, Cillian inched through on his belly too, not wanting to be left out.

Opie ran to the edge of the slope. There was a ten-foot drop of loose stones to the train track. Xu, Jackson and Cillian followed. Cillian stood too close to the edge and Opie could hear stones rattling down the edge, dislodged by his feet.

"Oh no," said Xu and pointed.

A little girl in a grubby princess dress was sliding

down the slope. She was still clutching her fairy wand, now broken and dirty

"Stay here," Xu told Opie. "There are trains every few minutes. It's too dangerous."

"No no wait!" Opie grabbed Xu as he took his first step down the gravelled slope. Just one step dislodged loose stones that bounced towards Olive, sending her sliding faster down the slope.

In the distance Opie saw a train heading towards them. If Olive kept sliding downwards, she was going to land in front of it.

"Olive!" Xu got on to his hands and knees and called softly down to the toddler. "Can you climb up? Can you come up here?"

Olive tried to reach up with one hand, but the movement loosened the stones, sliding her further towards danger.

Across the train tracks, at the top of the slope on the opposite side, Opie saw ten girls and boys in yellow fluorescent vests rubbing their faces and looking confused. A couple were holding sticks and looked injured. Mulaki was running towards them, together with a man and a woman who rushed at one of the footballers and hugged him tightly. They caught sight of Olive and broke out of the hug. Her parents, Opie guessed. They started shouting Olive's name and waving at her.

Squealing with delight, Olive scrambled down the slope. Towards her parents on the other side of the track.

"Stop, Olive love, don't move!"

Olive didn't understand. She gave them a little wave.

OPIE
Help.

She threw the thought up to the sky.

Opie couldn't mumble this in her usual way. She had to be assertive. She thought about what she needed, in one clear thought.

Mulaki spotted Opie staring up at the sky, mouth open, concentrating. As far as Mulaki knew, Opie could only talk to insects. So what was the girl up to?

Opie was listening to the hundreds of birds flying above London. It was chaos in her head. Birds had to think very quickly. If they didn't, they'd be splattered against skyscrapers or sucked into plane engines.

She was hunting for a flock of birds that could work together. And she'd found it. She could hear seven or eight individual birds all thinking in harmony, like eight speakers all playing the same song. Opie concentrated on inserting herself into this tightly meshed gang.

A V-shaped formation of geese flew above the train tracks and swooped down towards Olive in a fast, powerful dive.

"No!" Olive's parents shouted as the birds pressed their wide webbed feet on to Olive's back, beating their wings hard.

Mulaki understood. "They're holding her in place."

Opie looked up, panting slightly, and smiled at Xu. "You can get her now."

Xu scrabbled down the slope on his stomach as fast as he could, tearing his velvet culottes. Jackson grabbed Xu's ankles as he slid past. As Jackson slid down the slope on *his* stomach, Cillian grabbed Jackson's ankles too. The three were just the right length for Xu to seize Olive.

There was a cheer from the other side of the train tracks, drowned out by the train speeding past. Olive pressed her hands tightly against her ears as Xu passed her upwards towards Jackson.

"Got her?" Xu shouted.

"Yeah," panted Jackson, passing Olive upwards. "Hello Princess." Olive hit him gently on the head with her broken fairy wand.

Opie crawled towards Cillian, reaching him just in time to take Olive from his arms. Olive tapped Opie on the head with her wand in a small 'hello'.

The geese waddled up the side of the slope, pecking Xu and the boys along their bodies, checking if they were edible.

"Ow."

"Ow."

"Ow ow. Opie? Can you help?"

OPIE
Thank you! So kind!
Would you mind not pecking the people, maybe please?

GOOSE #1
Are they food?

OPIE
No. Friends not food.

GOOSE #2
Pah.

The birds flew away. Opie and Cillian helped Jackson and Xu up the slope, where they lay flat on their backs, recovering. Olive sat on Xu's chest, determined to push her fairy wand up his nose.

"Well done!" Mulaki was shouting across the track. Opie gave her a weary wave.

XU

Welcome to The Resistance, dull girl.

Opie made the complicated R shape with her fingers at him. Xu did it back.

"See! It's catching on!" he said.

"I was doing it sarcastically."

Xu shook his head, pretending to be annoyed. "You're out of The Resistance again. You lasted two seconds, well done."

Jackson reached over a weary hand and patted Opie's shoulder. "Well done." And Opie could not remember the last time she felt so *special*.

As they were clambering back through the wire fence, Cillian turned to Opie. "My birthday?" he said.

"Oh . . . yes?"

"It's at Brockwell Lido, in two Saturdays' time. If you wanna come."

"Cool, yeah, sure, whatever, that'd be cool."

Opie beamed when Cillian wasn't looking.

She was going to write *Opie Jones: Mind Reader* on ALL her school books.

MALCOLM

And does The Resistance make you feel good about yourself?

OPIE

Yeah, sure. It's nice to, I don't know? Like, belong?

MALCOLM

You don't know? You seem uncertain.

OPIE

I ... maybe. I dunno. I just talk like this.

MALCOLM

I see. Do you surround yourself with bigger, more confident, mercurial characters?

OPIE

What does mercurial mean?

MALCOLM

It's like capricious.

OPIE

Oh, okay, thanks.

MALCOLM

Do you know what capricious means?

OPIE

No.

CHAPTER EIGHTEEN

MALCOLM THE GUINEA PIG GAZED AT OPIE GRAVELY from the armchair, his front paws tucked neatly beneath him. Sitting cross-legged on the floor, Opie felt, yet again, like she'd said the wrong thing.

To Opie's surprise, Jackson was a very good manager: organised and hard-working. She had so many customers that she was fitting some appointments in before school. He had found Opie another client, a guinea pig called Malcolm who was pulling his fur out in clumps. The vet said it was stress. Opie was determined to understand Malcolm's emotions and help him to feel calmer. Unfortunately, Malcolm was convinced that *she* was the patient, and Opie now seemed to have a tiny therapist.

She felt guilty taking money as they spent the hour

talking about *her* feelings, but Malcolm seemed to enjoy it. The bald patch on his bottom was growing furry again.

Malcolm glanced at the clock.

MALCOLM
We're reaching the end of our time, Opie. We'll examine your feelings of inadequacy next week.

OPIE
I ... what? I don't feel inadequate.

MALCOLM
Do you know what inadequate means?

OPIE
Yes thank you. I do!

Opie inflated the bubble in her head, meaning Malcolm couldn't read her thoughts any more. She had become very good at this now and regularly did it when Malcolm was being patronising. Aunt Connie had got a second budgie who was no cleverer than the first; Opie frequently inflated the bubble in her head when she visited and the chat became unbearable.

Malcolm examined his little paw, looking smug. He couldn't read her mind but he knew he'd hit a nerve.

Feeling inadequate, Opie said goodbye to Malcolm's owner, passed on a message about a BBC documentary that Malcolm wanted to watch and pocketed her fee.

School was a lot more fun these days, after Opie's heroics with Olive and the geese. Cillian was much nicer to her. Or at least, he seemed to dislike her a lot less. Some days, from a distance, they could even look like friends.

The Resistance had taken Opie on as a full member and were training her up. Opie's greatest skill seemed to be with birds.

Mulaki said that they still didn't know what Varling

was planning. They knew his ultimate goal was to turn Saint Francis of Assisi into a warehouse staffed with children, but they didn't know exactly how he would do it.

Varling didn't mind them knowing his plans, as Xu said darkly, "We can't tell anyone, we'd give away that we're mind readers too!"

Opie headed for school past the Varling cinema where Troy worked and looked in the window for him, as had become her habit. He was a new addition to the friends she greeted on her walk to school. They made The Resistance sign at each other and it made her feel like a spy.

Opie headed down the road where the older lady with the tomato plants lived but she wasn't outside. Opie hovered for a moment outside her garden and checked her watch. She was right on time. She was about to keep walking when she saw the lady inside her house.

Opie raised her hand to wave, but the lady stared at her with an unfriendly face and gave her a thin, unenthusiastic smile. Feeling hurt, Opie slowly turned away and carried on walking. That was odd. She couldn't think what she'd done to annoy the lady.

Opie brightened when she saw her policeman friend carrying his bike out of his house as usual. She stopped and held his garden gate open for him with her usual morning salute.

"Thank you," he said shortly, without his usual salute back.

Opie dropped her hand from her forehead, feeling silly.

"You go to Saint Francis then?" he said, nodding at her backpack, which had the school badge on.

"Yes?" said Opie, realisation dawning.

"Shame," he said. "I went there. It used to be a nice school."

"It still is," said Opie, feeling defensive.

"Really?" he said, and took out his phone. It was open on an article about the damage done by the Saint Francis of Assisi football club. There was no mention of Opie saving Olive's life, but instead lots of graphs and pie charts showing how over half of the school was now excluded or expelled.

Opie took the phone off him and read on. There were quotes from parents of young children saying that they were trying to move house in order to send their kids to a 'better' school. They said that they were terrified of their children going to such a violent 'institution'.

There was an interview with other people who lived near Saint Francis of Assisi who said, because of all the fighting, they were scared to go out at night. They drew their curtains, locked their doors and had cameras and security devices all over the outside of their house to keep them safe.

Opie realised the article was on Varling's website. He'd really laid on the drama. She didn't recognise her own school from these descriptions.

"It's not like that," she said, clearing her throat to hide how upset she felt.

"Isn't it?" The policeman took back his phone. "I spent all yesterday helping to clear the broken glass and damaged cars on the high street. Your football team did thousands of pounds' worth of damage. People got hurt. Make sure you don't get dragged into any of that nonsense, okay?" He gave her a salute and cycled away.

Opie hurried off, feeling like everyone was staring at her. As she approached her school, she could see groups of people standing outside. A few were filming the school with their phones, as if drama might break out at any minute.

Feeling shy, Opie took off her backpack with its identifying school badge and hugged it to her chest so no one could see it. She darted through a group of adults, catching a glimpse of a thin-faced blonde woman that she recognised from Leo's bullying in the park. Definitely one of Varling's mind readers. What a hypocrite, Opie thought, standing with all these people, pretending she was anxious when *she* was causing the problem.

Opie hurried through the school doors just in time for the bell for assembly, chucking her backpack in her form room as she passed. She might bring a different bag to school tomorrow, she thought. The school badge felt like walking around with a dirty word written on her back.

Opie sneaked into the main hall. It was a big room, usually full of a thousand students so you could duck in late without being noticed. However, today fewer than half the kids were left.

"Thank you for joining us, Ms Jones," the Head, Ms Boutros, said drily from her lectern. Opie gave an apologetic smile and scurried across the hall to join Jackson and Cillian, and sat with what was left of her class.

She looked across the almost empty hall, catching Monsieur Lunarca's eye. He was eyeing the vast expanse of floor which was usually covered in cross-legged students.

"Ten left!" Monsieur Lunarca mouthed at Opie, pointing at his shrunken class and giving an expressive shrug. Opie returned the shrug, feeling like a liar because she knew exactly what had happened.

Opie's class was down to twelve people. Ms Mollo was whispering to a colleague with a worried look on her face. Opie tried to listen, but the amplified voice of the Head made it hard.

Jackson nudged her gently and whispered, "Ms Mollo's worried that excluded kids won't catch up in time for exams."

"She shouldn't worry. We'll all be packing boxes by Christmas," Opie whispered back.

Jackson made a sad face. Opie was pleased to see he was still wearing the new friendship bracelet she had given him, after swearing she'd tied it around a mug handle and not her big toe this time.

Maybe she should give Cillian a friendship bracelet too? She didn't want him to feel left out and he had been much nicer to her lately. She started thinking about colours and threads instead of listening to Ms Boutros. But suddenly, a word from the stage made her sit up and pay attention.

Ms Boutros had said the name *Varling*.

"What?" she muttered to Jackson, who hadn't been listening either.

"Mr Varling is a very successful businessman," Ms Boutros was saying. "In fact, he . . . bought our local library."

She had a funny look on her face. Varling had

bought the library and turned it into shops, and Opie doubted Ms Boutros thought that was cool. There was a "boo!" in a French accent from the side of the room. Monsieur Lunarca *definitely* didn't think that was cool.

Ms Boutros ignored the heckle. "Mr Varling contacted me to offer his condolences for the difficult term we're experiencing."

She sighed and patted her hair into place. Opie thought that it must be stressful to be head of a school where all your pupils turn into mind-controlled thugs.

"And he thought maybe the remaining pupils deserved a treat," Ms Boutros went on.

A quiet "oooooooooh!" ran around the room as the kids got excited at the thought of a treat. Opie, Jackson and Cillian exchanged wary looks. Monsieur Lunarca folded his arms and looked stubborn.

"So Mr Varling has offered to take you all to the zoo for a day trip, to show our community and the media . . ." (clearly Ms Boutros had read that article too) ". . . that Saint Francis of Assisi pupils CAN behave themselves. Because you can, can't you?" she appealed, looking desperate.

There was a murmur around the room as everyone promised they could and indeed *would* behave themselves.

Opie felt sorry for her fellow pupils, knowing that most of them would not behave themselves at the zoo. It wouldn't be their fault, but they'd still pay the price. It was so very unfair.

At least she could report back to The Resistance. She knew what the final piece of Varling's plan was now.

"So I invited Mr Varling and his assistant here today so we could say thank you properly, with traditional Saint Francis of Assisi politeness!" said Ms Boutros in a firm tone of voice, staring at them all very hard. Her meaning was clear. 'Please oh please be polite or it's cabbage in the canteen forever.'

Two people joined the Head onstage: an expensively-dressed blond man with very blue eyes and a woman with lilac-coloured hair, a nose ring and – this would be relevant – wide-legged trousers.

Opie hadn't seen either of them before, but she sensed instantly that the lilac-haired woman was a mind reader and Varling was not. From spending time with The Resistance, she just KNEW when she was around someone with special abilities. She wondered if they could tell she had similar abilities, or if she was different to human telepaths.

The lilac-haired woman ran her eyes around the room, pausing for ages on Opie's class, and staring at every face in turn. Opie inflated the protective bubble in her head, glad that she'd put in the hours of practice. The woman clearly sensed that there was someone with abilities, but she couldn't place her. This delighted Opie.

Varling was droning on. It sounded like he was saying anything that popped into his head. Opie suspected that his speech wasn't the reason he had come. The lilac-haired mind reader was.

Sure enough, as Varling waffled on about the importance of comfortable shoes and not throwing your packed lunch at giraffes (Ms Boutros looked offended), the woman got a familiar vacant look on her face. She was concentrating hard.

There was squirming among the youngest kids at the front of the room. Now they were getting agitated, pushing each other and starting to bicker.

"Children," Ms Mollo hissed fiercely, but they ignored her. Usually no one ignored Ms Mollo, especially when she used that tone.

The shoving grew more violent until kids were wrestling on the floor. Monsieur Lunarca hurried to separate them. Shockingly, one of the tiny fighters wheeled round, pigtails swinging, and shoved *him*.

There was a gasp from the room. The girl was only six but big for her age, and Monsieur Lunarca was small and round, so her shove made him stumble back.

Opie stood up in outrage. Monsieur Lunarca was her favourite teacher! This telepath woman wanted to pick on little kids? Well, maybe she'd like to pick on someone even smaller.

Since the beginning of assembly, Opie had been aware of quiet tuneful singing nearby.

All things bright and beautiful, all creatures great and smaaaaaaall . . .

This singing was exactly like the voice Opie heard doing Star Wars sound effects at home. *This* voice clearly lived in the school walls, because it was singing a hymn they sang in assembly.

OPIE
Hello friend, got a minute?

The kids pushing and shoving each other on the ground looked up at the first screams.

The lilac-haired woman was hopping around the stage with one foot held high in the air, squealing in panic. A large and tuneful rat had run straight up her trouser leg. Her concentration was well and truly broken.

The kids stopped fighting at once. They helped each other up and retrieved shoes that only a second ago they had used to hit each other.

"Are you OK, Misshure Lunarca?" asked the little

kid who'd pushed him over. "Did you trip?"

Looking puzzled, Monsieur Lunarca let her help him to his feet.

Varling hurried offstage. The woman followed, still hopping and shrieking. That rat had really committed to his job.

"That was too obvious," Opie whispered to Jackson. "Varling got overconfident."

Jackson nodded, grinning. "You should work with rats more."

Cillian peeked around Jackson. "Excuse me, can you two stop whispering and leaving me out for just one second? Do you think you could do that?"

"Sorry, you're further away, I can't whisper to you," Opie apologised. "I thought Jackson would pass on what I was –"

"Yeah whatever." Cillian sat back irritably.

They filed back to their form room for their English lesson. Ms Mollo seemed distracted. Opie noticed a few more absent pupils.

"Ms Mollo," she said, raising her hand. "Where are Lottie and Amit? Have they been fighting too?"

"No," Ms Mollo said wearily, looking down the register. "Their parents were worried that the school wasn't safe. So they're sending them somewhere else."

"Do you think more parents will do that, Ms Mollo?" asked Cillian in a small voice.

Ms Mollo gave him a rare smile. "I hope not, Cillian. But there's nothing we can do about it except behave well at the zoo and prove that Saint Francis of Assisi is a great school. Mr Varling has offered to bring some photographers to capture us at our best."

Jackson, Cillian and Opie smiled wanly.

"That'll be nice," said Opie. Meaning 'THIS WILL BE TERRIBLE OH NO SO VERY BAD.'

I've never been so glad to see sunrise. That was a long night. There was something HUGE digging all night next to my den. I don't know what it was but it sounded like a monster. I rolled myself tightly into a ball and prayed I'd live to see the morning.

I'm sorry, that was me.

CHAPTER NINETEEN

A LOVELY SUNNY SATURDAY AND HOW WAS OPIE spending it? Getting up at the crack of dawn to go and stand on a bridge in the middle of town. She yawned as she made herself a packed lunch in the kitchen.

There was a dramatic wail from upstairs. Violet was terrible in the mornings and wanted everyone to know it.

"It's *eeeeeaaaarly*!" Violet complained as she stumbled downstairs. She drooped over the kitchen table with a moan.

Harvey hurried down with wet hair and unruly eyebrows. He had to get up very early when he was filming *Highland Docs*, even at the weekend. Although, he said, the film crew fiddled with lights until noon, so he spent his mornings napping until the First Assistant Director found him.

"I'm looking forward to today," he announced. "It's the climax of that very complicated storyline of the two doctors who were enemies but are actually twins. Dr Ahmed has to break the news to them, over a dangerously blocked nose!"

Violet frowned at him sleepily. "*Your* nose, or . . .?"

"I'll call you at lunch and talk you through it," Harvey said, patting Violet affectionately on the head. "Why are you up so early, Opie?"

"I . . . am going to the special summer school for kids who prefer books to sunshine," said Opie, repeating the lie she had practised. "Can you drop me off at the train station?"

"Is that where it is?" said Violet.

"Umm . . ." said Opie, panicking. She hadn't thought about where this fake school would BE. "They . . . there's a BUS! From, from, from, from the station! So that's the reason for THAT!"

"Oh right, fair enough," said Harvey.

Both parents turned back to their morning coffee.

Opie breathed a sigh of relief. She would make the WORST spy.

Harvey dropped Opie off with four emergency-contact numbers and ten pounds for *emergencies*, he said, stressing that word.

"Dad, name ONE time I have ever been naughty," Opie said.

Harvey thought about it and admitted that she had a point. (Apart from right now with all the lying. Opie reminded herself, with a guilty twinge.)

She kissed her dad goodbye and he hurried off. As soon as he was out of view, Opie doubled back to her train platform. She wasn't being *that* reckless, she told herself, travel card sweaty in her hand. She was only travelling two stops unaccompanied by an adult. Then everything would be fine.

The 'adult' popped into her mind as the train pulled into South Bermondsey station.

XU

Well hello there, Animal Crackers.

Opie didn't *love* the nickname Xu had given her. It lacked dignity.

She and Xu travelled to Waterloo, shivering in the cold morning air. It was seven o'clock and the air still felt damp. Opie nearly lost Xu several times in the crush of people, who were all marching at top speed with their heads down, staring at their phones. Opie had a nasty feeling that if she tripped and fell, the tide of people would just wash over her. She kept a tight hold of Xu's coat, ignoring his tutting about creases.

They joined the rest of The Resistance on Waterloo Bridge. Mulaki told them to not attract attention, but that wasn't Xu's style.

"Watch this," he said.

In unison, hundreds of people below started skipping, their eyes still on their phones. Xu made them all jump up and down three times, do a little shimmy, and keep walking as if nothing had happened. It was like London was turning into a musical.

"Stop that, Xu," said Bear. "We're here to *help*. Like this."

Bear made a movement with his index fingers, redirecting two tangled streams of people. Instantly everyone moved more quickly past each other, with fewer commuters snapping, "Excuse *me*!"

Troy looked a bit constipated as he concentrated on the thousands of people below. His direction was very subtle, but Opie spotted the way people were suddenly walking slower, looking up and smiling at each other.

"Chasing away gloom," Mulaki said. "It's not flashy but it's important."

"Oh hello!" came a chirpy voice behind them.

Opie turned to see Jackson with a moody-looking Cillian.

"We were just passing," Jackson said smoothly. "Fancy seeing you here! Can we help?"

"If not that's cool, we'll go home again," said Cillian, grouchy with pillow marks all over his face.

Opie had spent months wishing they'd include her in their weekend plans and now they were gatecrashing hers! She tried not to look smug but she wasn't successful. Cillian scowled.

"You can be quiet," said Mulaki firmly. "We're trying to teach Opie."

"She's like the cleverest person in our school," said Jackson loyally, "so you'll be done very soon, I bet. Why don't you go to the Aquarium and practise on the sharks?"

Even Cillian brightened up at that, and The Resistance thought it was an awesome idea, until . . .

"Family group or school trip?" the girl on the ticket booth asked.

Mulaki stared at their mismatched group. "Hmmm, something in between?" she said.

"I'll charge you for school group, bit cheaper," said the girl, tapping the side of her nose and winking. The ticket price flashed up on her till and Mulaki physically recoiled.

Ten minutes later they were back on the bridge.

"Maybe," Jackson suggested, "you could sometimes use your powers for evil –"

"No."

"Light evil?"

"No."

"Just sometimes? Make a bit of money?"

Mulaki frowned. "No!"

"Not evil then, just not good," said Jackson. "A bit of card cheating?"

"A TV gameshow?" Cillian suggested.

"You know, you *could* . . ." Troy began, but fell silent at a look from his boss.

"Everyone be quiet," snapped Mulaki. "Let Opie practise."

"No pressure then," Opie murmured as everyone fell silent.

She looked around for some birds. This seemed to be her speciality, although she was so new to this that *speciality* felt like a bold word.

Meanwhile, the other Resistance members went on pushing happy thoughts into people's minds, driving out sadness and negativity. It sounded simple, but they were testing themselves by doing it on large groups of people at once and at increasing distances.

"This is what we'll be doing when your school go to

the zoo," Bear told Jackson and Cillian. "Varling's telepaths will be bombarding people's brains with rage, to make them fight, so we'll be sending them happy thoughts instead. We have to hope your schoolmates choose to be kind over angry. And that they don't scatter all over the zoo, cos that's a lot of ground to cover."

"And Opie will be helping too," said Troy. "Except with animals."

"Yeah, any idea how that'll work?" Xu asked the group.

Opie made a thinking face but this was a lie, she had NO thoughts. She'd tried to research it, reasoning that she couldn't be the ONLY animal telepath in the world. But, as Mulaki had pointed out, secret superheroes don't advertise online. Opie picked at the peeling paint on Waterloo Bridge, feeling left out. She couldn't do anything to help.

Cillian watched her, looking pleased to see she wasn't so cocky any more. She had been jubilant the day she'd saved Olive; Jackson had ridden around with her on his handlebars, singing superhero theme tunes and Cillian had cycled behind, furious and forgotten.

"Why are you even here, Dopey?" Cillian said maliciously. "It's not like you can actually DO anything useful – OW!"

Cillian flailed like he was trying to punch the wind.

"You okay?" Jackson said.

"Something bit me on the ear!" he wailed, looking around, confused

Four pairs of eyes looked at Opie. She hid behind her fringe, smirking. He wasn't bitten, he was *pecked*.

OPIE
Thanks.

SPARROW
No worries, pal.

While Cillian sulked, and Jackson watched The Resistance work on a particularly grumpy queue for the London Eye, Opie tried to chat to a couple of pigeons.

PIGEON #1

Can't stop, sorry mate. Catch you later, rush aar innit.

PIGEON #12

Dave! Dave!

PIGEON #9

Have a butcher's dahn here, is that a bakery van with its doors open?

PIGEON #12

Anyone seen Dave?
Dave!

Pigeons, it turned out, were really busy, and weren't big fans of chatting to strangers. Opie gave up. She peeked over the edge of the bridge and watched a portly man stop and mop his brow. He shifted his backpack on his back, wincing at the weight.

Opie wanted to cheer him up somehow. Her dad had that backpack.

Across the river she saw a flock of starlings sunning themselves on the roof of a building. She concentrated hard, feeling that stupid look slide across her face.

OPIE
Hello. Um. Have you got a minute?

Hundreds of small birds across the river turned their heads to Opie and cocked them to one side, listening politely.

Down at street level, the man pocketed his handkerchief with a sigh. He'd better keep going or he'd be late, it would be a busy weekend shift at the restaurant and . . .

He suddenly lost his train of thought. Hundreds of starlings were swooping towards him, banking sharply, moving in unison. They were so densely packed they turned the air black. Then they spread out and swooped upwards again, looking like a vast, speckled cape flung through the sky. Around him, other people stopped and stared at the small miracle in front of them.

"That's a murmuration," said Cillian, the know-it-all.

"It's *Opie's* murmuration." Troy pointed at Opie, who was staring at the sky, one hand slightly raised.

Opie was concentrating harder than she ever had before, her eyes fixed on the giant flock of birds. But she could only hold on to that focus for another few seconds before it was gone. The birds drifted away and the crowds below the bridge made disappointed *awww* noises and went back to rushing around.

"Well done," said Troy.

"That was amazing," said Bear sincerely.

"But what's the point?" Cillian asked. "No offence, but –"

"Wonder," Mulaki told him firmly. "Moments of wonder and awe that make people look up from their lives and feel amazed at the natural world. People in big cities can forget that the whole world isn't concrete and human design. Opie just reminded them of that."

Opie beamed. Mulaki made her feel so special.

"All right, Attenborough, keep your khakis on," Xu muttered. Cillian sniggered.

The Resistance went back to work while Opie slumped to the ground for a rest. She was utterly drained and glad to share a can of fizzy drink with Jackson. He asked her questions about how she talked to the animals and was fascinated by her answers. So was Cillian, although he pretended to be on his phone.

On the other side of the bridge, a Mercedes with blacked-out windows stopped in the middle of the road. Cars behind hooted, but the driver stretched a languid hand out of the window and waved at them to drive round.

In the Mercedes, Max Inkelaar stared at Opie, tuning in to scraps of her conversation with the boys. He smiled to himself. An *animal* mind-reader. How amusing, in a tacky, novelty sort of way.

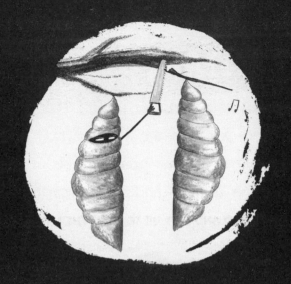

Day three.
It's quite hot in here.
And this one won't. Stop. Humming.

CHAPTER TWENTY

OPIE SIGHED AND GOT UP TO HELP THE WASP THAT WAS flying repeatedly into her bedroom window.

OPIE
Hang on, calm down.

WASP
Why is the sky so hard?

OPIE
Stop panicking, it's going to be okay.

WASP
Something is very wrong!

Opie opened the window and used a book to gently guide the wasp towards it. It finally found the open window and flew away, marvelling at its own ingenuity.

WASP

I've made it, I'm FREEEEEEEE!! I'm so CLEVER.

"You're welcome," said Opie sarcastically, but the wasp was already a tiny dot in the sky.

Opie had noticed that when animals panicked, there was no talking to them. This was a concern, given that *everyone* would be panicking at the zoo. The stress was making her temper flare up. Small things like walking past a door and getting her pocket caught on the doorknob (which happened more than you'd think) were enough to make her explode with rage.

She was working on ways to stay calm because she didn't like this new, hot-tempered version of herself. She had practised for days on inflating the imaginary bubble in her head, to shut out all the animal thoughts and get some peace and quiet, and could now do it instantly. Also, she had spent hours making a friendship bracelet for Cillian in time for his birthday party today. It was green, white and gold, and looked very Irish. She thought he'd like it, depending on his mood.

Opie returned to her notebook. Mulaki had told her to assemble a crack team of animals to work with at the zoo. This was not easy. Opie's list currently looked like this:

- Malcolm (bad for my self-confidence, but fits in pocket)
- School rat (sings all the time but also fits in pocket)
- Pigeons (never listen)
- Budgies (dimmer than a broken lightbulb)
- Margot (unhelpful, moody, will eat team members 1-4, will not fit in pocket)

Cursing, Opie brushed her hair, wincing as the brush hit the knots. She was in such a bad mood today. She needed to shake herself out of it before Cillian's birthday party. Loads of her schoolmates would be there, including excluded and expelled ones, and she wanted to talk to them all in case they remembered anything helpful about their experience of being mind controlled. Apparently a lot of them had been sent to anger management and counselling by their worried parents. Opie wanted to tell them to save their money. Their kids were fine. It was all Varling and his mind readers.

Opie had saved up her earnings from her animal clients and bought a swimming costume. It was black with long rainbow-coloured laces for straps and she loved it. She worried about the long elastic straps coming undone, but when she tried it on Violet had triple-knotted them and promised they were secure.

She put her clothes over her swimming costume and headed for Cillian's party at the lido. It was another baking hot day, and she couldn't wait to get in the pool. She'd never been to a private party at the lido. It was always crammed, and she had to be careful of bigger kids running and doing bombs into the water. That wouldn't happen today.

When Opie got there, the pool was full and there

wasn't much barbecue food left. She double-checked her invitation. It looked like Cillian had invited his favourite people to come earlier, then people he liked less, such as Opie, later in the day.

She regretted spending so much time working on his friendship bracelet now.

Opie looked around for Jackson. An inflatable ball hit her in the face.

"Oops! Sozzlecopter!" Cillian said with a cheeky grin. He and Jackson were playing catch in the deep end.

Jackson waved. "Opie! Come play! We'll go a bit shallower so you can stand up."

Opie quickly took off her shorts and T-shirt, a little shy in her swimming costume. Then she slipped into the pool towards her friend and frenemy, hopping on the very tips of her toes to join them near the deep end. The water had an oily sheen of suntan lotion on the surface and she had to pick her way through kids to reach Jackson and Cillian.

"Hi, hey there, hi!" She waved shyly at various people as she passed them. So many kids had been excluded from school. It was nice to see them all again.

"Is this shallow enough for you, Opie?" Jackson asked.

He was much taller, so he was standing easily. Cillian was hopping on his tiptoes too, but pretending he wasn't almost out of his depth.

"Yeah, I'm cool!" Opie lied.

Cillian snorted meanly. "Hardly," he said. He and Opie really didn't bring out each other's best side.

Jackson, of course, was oblivious. He laughed and threw the ball so it bounced gently off Cillian's head. "C'mon grumpy."

They started throwing the ball around, though Cillian never threw it to Opie, so she bobbed in the pool, pointed toes cramping, while she watched.

"Cillian, throw it to Opie more!" Jackson chided gently.

"Sure, I am though!" Cillian lied, throwing it at Jackson again.

"Whatever," said Opie, flatly. She wasn't usually so rude but Cillian was aggravating her.

Cillian brushed behind Opie and tugged her hair. "Oops, sorry!"

So childish, Opie thought. Pulling my hair. Didn't even hurt.

They played catch a little longer, with Cillian being deliberately polite to Opie and throwing the ball to her repeatedly. Two could play that game, she thought. She thanked him elaborately each time.

'See, Cillian, we can SHARE our friend,' she nearly said, but bit her tongue. No point starting a squabble when they were having a nice day.

Her toes were still cramping, so after ten minutes she kicked towards the stepladder and hauled herself out of the pool.

As she straightened up, she felt a tugging on her hair. She couldn't hold her head up properly, it was being pulled to one side. She hadn't noticed in the water but now she realised that her hair was tangled in her swimsuit straps.

Opie reached her hands around her back, first stretching above her head then trying from below. As she struggled, she went on her tiptoes and started spinning in a slow circle. She didn't realise she was doing that until the giggling and pointing started. Opie hated giggling and pointing, it was always mean, and it was extra bad when it was aimed at her.

Red-faced, head on one side, she hurried back to her towel and sat down with a thump. She knew what had happened now. Cillian had brushed past her a minute ago, when she was smirking at Jackson. That gentle tug... he wasn't just pulling her hair, he had sneakily tied her hair and her long rainbow straps together, and now she was stuck.

Opie had thought they were having a nice day.

Grimacing, she tugged her hair loose as quickly as possible, hot with pain and embarrassment. She glanced up and saw something that made her even madder.

Cillian was pointing at her now with big, exaggerated gestures, clearly telling Jackson that 'Dopey got tangled in her costume like a wally and everyone saw and OMG it was so embarrassing for her'. Jackson was laughing guiltily, hand over his mouth, turning his back so Opie wouldn't see. But she saw.

Cillian pulled himself out of the pool and did an impression of Opie on tiptoes, struggling with her arms behind her back. He smirked at her. The blush in

Opie's cheeks switched from embarrassment to rage. She was so furious she couldn't think straight.

It was like her brain was *buzzing* with fury.

OPIE
Come here.

There was a strange noise from the other side of the wall that ran around the lido. A humming noise, growing so loud it could be heard over the sound of everyone in the pool. A swarm of big, fat flying ants rose into view, moving in a thick, angry cloud. It was just how Opie's brain felt.

She didn't ask the ants to do anything. She TOLD them.

OPIE
Get him.

In a split second, the swarm swooped and descended on Cillian in a cloud of hard, buzzing bodies. He disappeared, shrieking.

People screamed, pushing past each other to get away. Jackson backed away, a look of horror on his face. Lifeguards raced towards Cillian, not knowing what to do, swatting uselessly at a single ant here and there.

"Push him in the water!" a deep voice commanded.

Obediently the lifeguards shoved Cillian into the lido. The people in the water yelped in fright and raced towards the steps.

But it worked. The ants flew away and the lifeguards could fish Cillian out of the pool. He was crying and covered in red marks.

Opie inhaled sharply. She didn't know how long she had been holding her breath, but she felt dizzy. She sat on a step and hugged her towel around herself, her head drooping until her forehead rested on her knees. She peeked out from under her fringe and watched the receptionist wrap Cillian in a towel and order the lifeguards to send for an ambulance.

"I didn't know ants bit," she whispered, like an apology and a confession.

It was so quiet and she was almost alone in the lido. Everyone else had run away or was helping Cillian.

Calm, measured footsteps walked towards her. She kept her head down, hiding behind her long, thick, wet hair.

"That was something."

It was the voice that had told the lifeguards to push Cillian in the water. Opie peered up at the man standing in front of her. She could tell instantly that he was a mind reader. She didn't recognise him so she inflated the bubble in her head to prevent him from reading her mind.

She saw him frown slightly. It was clear he now had no

idea what she was thinking. She kept her face smooth, determined that he couldn't read her face either.

"So," he said. "How old are you?"

"Ten."

"Clever."

Opie fought a smile that tugged at the edges of her mouth. She loved to be told she was clever, even by someone who was almost certainly evil. She didn't feel proud of herself for that.

"Tell me, clever girl, why can't I read your mind?"

Opie gave a shrug and no further information. She could tell he was annoyed but trying to hold his temper.

He fussily brushed the step beside her and sat down. "Are your parents rich?" he asked.

Opie was not expecting that question. "Uhhhh, no?" she said cautiously.

"Well, one day you might need money," he said. "Life is full of unpleasant surprises and sometimes only money will dig you out of a hole. If that day comes, here you go." And handed her a business card.

Opie didn't want to take the card but . . . anything could happen to Dr Ahmed. The *Highland Docs* surgery was an incredibly dangerous place. If Harvey's character was eaten by wolves or hit by a falling helicopter (both likely on that show) they'd have no money again.

She slowly reached up and took the card off him.

MAX INKELAAR

Logistics

VARLING ENTERPRISES

Sirens wailed in the distance, getting closer. Opie thought about how Cillian's parents would feel when they saw him and she felt sick.

"We would appreciate you," Max Inkelaar said and extended a hand for her to shake. "We're not rude like Xu."

Xu *was* rude. So Opie shook Max Inkelaar's hand.

Max walked away. Opie watched him pass a shivering Cillian being led to the ambulance without a second look, keeping the bubble firmly inflated in her head.

MALCOLM

Wow. That's awful.

OPIE

Is that all you've got? Nothing helpful about my feelings?

MALCOLM

Some people are allergic to insect bites.

OPIE

I didn't even know ants bit! And he isn't allergic cos if he was he'd have an EpiPen and there'd be a note about it in our form room.

MALCOLM

That doesn't make it –

OPIE

I know that doesn't make it okay! I'm just saying.

MALCOLM

Our time is nearly up.

OPIE

Great.

CHAPTER TWENTY-ONE

OPIE DID NOT WANT TO GO TO SCHOOL ON MONDAY MORNING. She felt guilty about Cillian. And even though her schoolmates didn't know the flying ants had been her fault, Jackson did. Would he even talk to her?

She wasn't a superhero. She was a terrible person.

Max Inkelaar's business card sat on her bedside table, propped up against her lamp. She would never contact him. She wasn't *that* bad, she thought. But she hadn't thrown it away either.

She skipped breakfast with her parents, who kept asking what had happened at Cillian's party as they'd heard vague rumours. Opie said she'd been in the toilet at the time, but she couldn't stand them to hear them wondering if Cillian was okay. Especially as she didn't know the answer.

Opie speed walked to school, marching past the people she usually greeted, stopping very briefly to kiss Margot on the head. Her arms ached from holding her backpack in her arms, trying to hide her Saint Francis of Assisi badge. She was feeling so many layers of shame, like a sad onion.

When she reached her form room, Jackson was already at his desk. He waved at Opie cheerfully, as if nothing had happened.

Opie slid uncertainly into the seat next to him. "Have you seen Cillian?" she asked quietly.

"Oh my God." Jackson looked at her, eyes wide. "He looks gross. Spots all over. Will you make me another friendship bracelet? I've decided I want a full arm of them."

"They're bites not spots," said Opie. "Is he okay?"

"I was thinking royal blue, white and gold?" said Jackson. "For the bracelet."

Opie tried again. "I texted him but he never replied. I texted him a lot. I guess I understand him not wanting to talk to me."

"He'll have to talk to you eventually," said Jackson.

"You think?"

"He can't ignore you at school until it's time for university or whatever."

Opie stared at Jackson. She *had* told him about Varling's plan to turn the school into a warehouse and the students into warehouse workers. But she realised he hadn't been listening.

Opie was surprised to find she missed Cillian. He was much better at retaining information.

Still, Jackson could always surprise her.

As Ms Mollo talked at the front of the class, Jackson turned to Opie with a gleam in his eye. She thought he'd had another idea about his bracelet. She wasn't expecting him to come up with an idea that was sensible and yet scared her silly.

"That thing you do, where mind readers can't read your mind?" he said.

"The bubble thing?"

"Yeah, that!"

"Jackson and Opie, are you TALKING?" Ms Mollo's eyes were suddenly on them.

"No!" Jackson said.

"Yes," Opie admitted.

"You need to teach it to everyone, before the zoo trip," Jackson went on, when Ms Mollo resumed teaching.

"What?"

"It's the only way everyone can defend themselves, right?"

"I guess . . ."

"It'll help The Resistance."

Opie swallowed, her throat suddenly dry. "Can I write it down or . . ."

"No Opes," said Jackson. "You'll have to teach them, like – that."

Jackson nodded at Ms Mollo who, unfortunately, had stopped teaching again and was staring at them in a very detention-y way.

At break time, Jackson persuaded Opie to come out into the yard.

A woman was loitering by the fence, on the street outside the school. She looked like she was engrossed in her phone. Opie nudged Jackson and pointed.

"Telepath," she mouthed.

A scuffle suddenly broke out between two boys near the woman. They were grabbing each other's shirts, shoving each other back and forth. Soon they stumbled and knocked over a girl from the lower years, who started crying. The girl's older sister then charged into the fight to smack both the boys and make them apologise.

Opie saw the woman smile to herself.

The football coach sprinted forward to separate the three pupils. There were a lot more teachers patrolling the yard at break time now, and fights were getting broken up more quickly.

Maybe no one will be excluded this time, Opie thought hopefully.

"Billy's bleeding," Jackson said.

One of the fighting boys looked like he'd lost a tooth. Opie sighed. Blood meant exclusion. Teachers would need reflexes like wild animals on the zoo trip if they had any chance of breaking up fights before Varling's photographers got shots of Saint Francis students brawling and traumatising a load of penguins.

It would be so helpful if she could teach her

schoolmates the bubble technique, Opie thought miserably. But there was no way to do it which didn't involve her standing up and talking in public – her stomach lurched – in front of hundreds of kids.

Back off.

CHAPTER TWENTY-TWO

IN A HORSE-RIDING CENTRE, OPIE WAS STRUGGLING. SHE was staring intently at a horse. But it was staring back even more intently. If she'd been feeling sensitive, she might have said it was hostile.

HORSE
I said. Back. Off.

Opie was struggling to concentrate. Last night, her parents had been unusually quiet. At dinner, Violet had arranged Harvey's food into the shape of a hedgehog. She only did things like that when it was someone's birthday, and it wasn't Harvey's birthday – thankfully, because he'd had a gloomy face on all night and that is not how you should feel on your birthday.

Opie had asked them both if they were okay and they'd said, "Yes, fine!" with bright smiles and sad eyes. She was not convinced. So she went to bed.

In the middle of the night Opie had woken up needing a glass of water. There was an empty glass on the kitchen table, as if someone else had been up in the night, and a thick stack of papers held together with metal clips. Opie recognised the papers as a *Highland Docs* script.

She'd flicked the light on and started reading. Dr Ahmed was going out to an emergency case up a mountain and – in a frankly unlikely chain of events – his car broke down and he smashed his phone, so he set off on foot and then fell over and broke his leg. And now night was coming, he could hear wolves howling and they were getting closer . . .

"And then what?" Opie muttered to herself.

She had reached the last page. Dr Ahmed was still lying in a ditch, thinking of all the women he had loved. This was taking a while and his time would've been better spent on a tourniquet.

No wonder Harvey was so sad. If Dr Ahmed was

eaten by a wolf, he would be out of work. And then what would Opie's family do for money?

Opie crept back to bed, but didn't fall asleep for ages. She lay awake staring at Max Inkelaar's business card. Last time her parents were out of work she hadn't been able to help them. This time, perhaps, she could.

Now, at the horse-riding centre, Opie was having to keep the bubble inflated in her head whenever she was near a member of The Resistance. She hoped that by the next episode Dr Ahmed would stop daydreaming about his messy love life and drag himself to safety before the wolves found him. Because she really didn't want to leave Mulaki and the others in the lurch.

This was such a distracting thought that she wasn't communicating very well with this horse; she was only managing to annoy him.

HORSE

You want trouble?
Cos I got trouble if you want trouble.

OPIE
Sorry.

HORSE
Get. Out. Of my head.

"All right, sorry sorry!" Opie backed away, bumping into Mulaki, who was engrossed in a very long To-Do list.

"Now Opie," Mulaki was saying. "There will obviously be a lot of wild animals at the zoo. Even the ones born in captivity will be more feisty than a friendly pony, but let's start you off easily – what's the matter?"

The 'friendly pony' bared his teeth at Opie, who quivered.

"See, he's smiling!" Mulaki was not an animal person.

Opie could feel Xu watching her. A big upside to being the

only animal telepath was that no one could tell how badly she was doing. Xu hated this. He was the most inconsistent member of The Resistance. Whenever he failed, everyone noticed. But so long as Opie kept a straight face and occasionally looked constipated, everyone believed she was making progress. She didn't want anyone to know she was struggling.

"Are you struggling?" Xu asked.

"How do you mean?" Opie asked, unwillingly.

Xu shrugged. "I think you're having problems communicating with that horse. And I know that happens if you have a lot on your mind. And I *know* you were at a birthday party last weekend where an ambulance was called for a kid. So I'm putting two and two together and wondering if there's anything you want to tell us?"

Troy, Bear and Mulaki were all listening now. Opie felt under pressure. So she haltingly told the story of Cillian and the flying ants.

"Opie." Bear was smiling. "We've *all* done things like this."

Opie squinted at him through her hair. "You have?"

"No one's proud of it, but it's like, the *first* thing you do when you discover you're a telepath," Bear said. "You use your powers to punish someone horrible. And then you're so disgusted with yourself, you make sure you never do it again."

Mulaki said, "Between us, we're responsible for a lot of traumatised siblings. We feel terrible about it –"

"I don't," Xu interrupted. "My brothers are horrible. They've got the personality of beans on toast."

Opie finally looked up. "Xu!" she tutted.

"All right, judgy-pants," said Xu comfortably. "None of *them* were covered in insect bites last time I checked, so –"

"Anyway." Mulaki glared at Xu. "The point is, with great power – "

" – comes great responsibility," Troy and Bear said in unison. "We know, it's Spider-Man."

"I'm still not sure," Opie said, worried. "I don't think I should be making myself *more* powerful if this is the damage I'm doing already."

Xu said kindly, "if the worst thing you can do is ants, I wouldn't worry. *We* are dabbling in mental, emotional turmoil. You're the cutesy fluff of The Resistance."

"I'm the *what* now?" Irritation replaced Opie's shame.

"Like those YouTube channels that show nothing but pictures of 'doggos' and cats confused by mirrors. Mindless cuteness," Xu explained.

Opie was so offended. She was a serious person, recruited to an underground rebellion who fought evil. She was NOT fluff.

Mulaki sent them off in pairs to practise again. But before they did, Opie wanted to tell them Jackson's idea about teaching her schoolmates how to block mind readers.

She was surprised that no one was more enthused about it.

"Is this because you're scared about using your powers?" Mulaki asked.

"No!" Opie said.

"You seem nervous," said Xu.

"Are you finding the training hard?" asked Troy, kindly but annoyingly.

This hurt Opie's feelings. She was usually the quickest in her class to learn new things and this was her first experience of not excelling. No wonder Jackson stopped listening if he found lessons as difficult as she found this stupid horse.

HORSE
You're stupid.

"You can't invent new things to do instead of your training," said Mulaki firmly.

"I'm not!" Opie insisted. "I think this could be really helpful. You can't be everywhere at once. Wouldn't it be better if students could defend themselves?"

The Resistance members looked sceptical.

"Why don't you have any faith in me?" Opie was furious now. "I've only been a mind reader for a couple of months and I'm catching up as fast as I can. But if we fail at the zoo, it's MY school that will be turned into a warehouse and MY small hands that will be packing boxes!"

She shook her hands at them.

"So are you not going to help me?" Opie demanded. "Am I going to have to give a talk in front of hundreds of my schoolmates, all by myself? I need a mind reader to know if their bubbles are working."

"Okay, okay," Mulaki sighed. "We'll help."

Which should have made Opie feel better, but it sounded like Mulaki was humouring her and that made her more angry. As if she WANTED to give a public speech! She'd rather talk to a *hundred* stupid horses than do that.

HORSE
Stand still.

OPIE

Oh sure. Why?

HORSE

I'm gonna kick you.

I don't handle stress very well to be honest, no. It affects my work very badly, my webs reflect my mood. I accidentally weave words like ARGH and UNBEARABLE in the middle of them. Creates an uncool vibe for everyone.

Honestly, I don't care. I've got bigger problems.

CHAPTER TWENTY-THREE

OPIE MARCHED AWAY FROM THE HORSE-RIDING CENTRE, thoroughly fed up. It was so important to teach the remaining people at her school how to protect their minds from Varling, and yet Mulaki and Xu thought she was only suggesting it to hide the fact that she was struggling to master mind reading. (She WAS struggling, of course. But that wasn't the point.)

Margot appeared out of nowhere and bounced lightly in front of her.

MARGOT
Man behind you.

OPIE
What? Who?

MARGOT

Dunno. Losing interest now.

And Margot trotted away, tail waving. Opie rolled her eyes. Mulaki had no idea how hard it was to assemble a 'crack team' of animals to work with when this was her best bet: a cat who literally couldn't care less.

Opie glanced behind her. It wasn't very subtle, but she needed to know who was following her. She instinctively inflated the bubble in her head.

"Hello," said Max Inkelaar. "Bad day?"

"I don't want to talk about it," said Opie. But she let him catch up with her and they walked on together.

They passed a young couple, who smiled at Opie and Max. They probably thought her and Max were father and daughter, thought Opie, not superhero and villain. What a ridiculous situation. It was hard to know how to behave. She wished she read comic books. That might have given her a guide.

"Anything I can do?" said Max mildly.

Opie laughed. "You want to help me? Help me

stop *your* boss from stealing my school and turning it into a warehouse where I'll have to work instead of getting educated?"

Max shrugged easily. "I don't like Varling either."

"Are you going to be at the zoo on Monday?" Opie asked.

He nodded.

"Do you think people might get hurt?"

"Maybe," said Max. "You should stay away."

Opie put her hands on her hips. "What and just leave my school friends to it? 'Good luck guys, hope you don't fall into the hippo tank'?"

Max shrugged. "I would."

Opie deflated the bubble in her head and thought, very clearly and deliberately, so Max could hear it: 'Yeah. YOU would.' Then she inflated it again, shutting him out of her thoughts.

Max frowned.

Opie stuck her hands in her pockets and walked onwards, humming casually. She would have whistled, but she couldn't whistle anything except one long, wobbling note and no one wanted to hear that.

She jumped at a quiet word from behind her as if it was a shout.

"Opie."

Mulaki was staring at Max and Opie, stony-faced. She had followed Opie out of the horse-riding centre, but had clearly been more subtle than Max as neither Margot nor Opie had noticed.

Max nodded at Mulaki, who nodded back, warm as two ice cubes.

"Bye Ms Jones, best of luck." Max gave Opie a small salute. She saluted back without thinking. Mulaki didn't look pleased.

"If you won't help me," said Opie, feeling reckless as Max walked away, "then maybe HE will."

"Fine," sighed Mulaki. "Maybe you're right. It would be helpful if the sponge heads could fend for themselves."

"Sponge heads?" said Opie.

"That is the politically correct term for non-telepaths, yes. Leaking thoughts everywhere like a wet sponge."

"Wow. Still *quite* rude?"

"Focus, Opie," said Mulaki. "We have a school assembly to plan."

Opie blinked. "I'm sorry, we what?"

The key to a good school assembly is structure. Keep it moving, keep it snappy. Don't mumble, don't tell them off for longer than ten minutes and always begin with a song. I personally like a hymn, but pop music is fine too. Opera – ambitious that early in the morning.

Good luck!

CHAPTER TWENTY-FOUR

"**R**OAD SAFETY?" MS BOUTROS BLINKED AT XU, BEAR and Troy.

"Mmm, yes." Xu adjusted his yellow high-visibility bib with distaste. "We're going round several schools in this area giving talks on road safety and . . . pavement politeness."

Bear gave Xu an exasperated look. "Teenagers make up the majority of pedestrian accidents, ma'am," he said. "Probably. So we like to brush up on the Green Cross Code: red man, green man, the basics, you know?" Troy nodded, looking casual, as if they spent most days chatting road safety and hadn't hastily googled it this morning.

"We had a dropout for this morning and wondered

if you'd like us to do a presentation to your school?" Xu added.

Bear, Troy and Xu had knocked on the staff-room door first thing that morning, while the Head and all the teachers were rubbing their eyes and drinking unpleasantly strong coffee. They were offering to take a school assembly at short notice, they seemed odd and their yellow high-visibility jackets were so new they had fold marks on them. But if they took assembly, Ms Boutros could spend half an hour marking and catching up with work. And, from the puppy dog eyes her colleagues were giving her, they would *love* that.

"And it's free," Bear added.

"Please please please," the maths teacher whispered, crumbling a biscuit in his hands with excitement.

"The hall is this way!" Ms Boutros hurried Bear, Xu and Troy along the corridor before they changed their minds. They were clearly the only people who didn't know about Saint Francis of Assisi's terrible reputation. Maybe they weren't the most hated school in the country, Ms Boutros thought. It had felt like it lately.

Opie was waiting at the side of the stage in the main hall, sorting through her carefully prepared flash cards. She'd been up late last night planning exactly how to explain the bubble technique to the school, stopping every ten minutes to hiccup with fear.

Harvey and Violet had tried to help. This was their speciality. But they were natural show-offs and it was impossible to explain to them what shyness felt like. Opie Jones was not a public speaker. She mumbled and got shy when talking to one human being. So several hundred people felt like an impossible task.

RAT
No, don't think like that. Audiences can smell fear.

OPIE
I think that's just rats.

RAT
Nope. There was a guest speaker here two

years ago, mumbled, lost his nerve, they sensed it. The chatting in the room was so loud you could hardly hear his footsteps as he ran away.

OPIE
I think I'm going to be sick.

She peeked out at the room as what was left of the school filed into the hall. Everyone was looking around curiously, noticing that there were no teachers sitting along the edge of the room as usual. Opie knew this had something to do with Bear and Troy outside the room. If any teacher came near, they would suddenly 'remember' that they had forgotten something and double back on themselves.

The children in the hall looked up, eyes wide, as Xu strode on to the stage, flinging his yellow high-visibility jacket aside. There were scattered *ooooh*s around the room at the sight of his lilac cape, which he swished elegantly.

"Have you noticed a lot more fighting and bad behaviour in the school?" he began.

Everyone in the hall nodded. Some people said "duh" and earned themselves a hard stare from Xu.

"And do you know why this is?" he asked.

A small kid near the front raised her hand confidently.

Xu pointed at her. "Yes?"

"Puberty," she announced.

"Good guess but no," he said. And as she seemed to want to argue about it, he pushed his next thoughts telepathically into everyone's heads.

XU
It's mind control.

A satisfyingly dramatic gasp ran through the room. Xu swished his cape, looking smug.

RAT
Oh, he's good, he's very good. Watch and learn, kid.

OPIE
Shush, you're making me nervous.

Now he had everyone's attention, Xu explained Varling's plans. Some kids looked delighted at the thought of no school, especially the ones with big exams coming up, so he had to go into detail about how hard warehouse work was until they were convinced. "Your hands get VERY cold," he said, several times.

He told them about the zoo and how Varling and his mind readers would make them riot, to get them all expelled, so he could shut the school down forever. The crowd looked horrified and Opie could see lots of O-shaped mouths.

She looked towards the back of the room, where Jackson was sitting with what remained of their class. From his gestures, she knew he was saying, "I knew this already," to anyone who would listen.

"What's more, a student at this school is also a mind reader," said Xu.

He didn't mention that Opie was an *animal* mind-reader. Opie scowled. She knew why. Xu still thought it was a daft super power. He wanted people to think she was a *proper* mind reader.

Lots of people turned and looked at Jackson. He

had an air of specialness about him. Of course anyone would think he was the superhero.

XU

She is going to teach you how to block someone from reading your mind. This is the only way you can keep yourself safe at the zoo.

The small kid at the front raised her hand again. Xu ignored it.

XU

It is a very important technique, and you will need to practise it constantly between now and Monday.

The small kid started waving her hand in a slow, sarcastic back and forth that Xu couldn't ignore any longer.

"What?" he said.

"Why don't we just not go to the zoo?" she asked, as if he was an idiot.

Backstage, Opie grinned. It was fun to watch someone being rude to Xu. He was always the one dishing it out.

"BE. CAUSE," said Xu slowly, "Varling would just try again. And again and again. Whereas if you can all prove that you can repel the efforts of twenty-five trained mind-readers, he will see that this school is too powerful to bring down!"

That was very inspiring and earned him some applause and a few fists punching the air.

XU

IF you can master the bubble technique.
Which you might not be able to.
That's up to Opie really.

Xu gestured at Opie to come out on stage. Opie stared at him and dropped a couple of flash cards.

RAT

That is the worst introduction I've ever seen.
Very ungenerous performer.

Opie thought the same as she trudged out on stage. It hadn't been the superhero announcement she'd hoped for.

There were many times she wished Xu and Mulaki had never chased her down an alleyway and changed her life forever. And this was one of those times.

Thanks for that. It was terrible, she thought, knowing Xu could hear it.

"*Opie Jones* is a mind reader?" she heard a voice mutter in the room.

XU
Yes, she is.

Out in the room, numerous people folded their arms and looked sceptical.

"Prove it then! Do the thing in our heads," a voice shouted.

Opie straightened herself up to her full, small height, imagining that she was Violet, and spoke clearly.

"I … don't have to prove anything," she said. "And I don't have time. We have ten minutes and I have to teach you something that will save this school. So be quiet and listen."

The whole room fell silent, except for one person.

"That's my friend," Jackson whispered proudly at the back of the room.

Opie hid her grin. "Right," she said. She looked at her flash cards, glad she'd spent most of the night rehearsing. Her parents always rehearsed.

"Imagine a bubble in your head," she told the room. "A small bubble. Then inflate it."

"Oi," someone shouted. "What does –"

"Inflate means make it bigger!" Opie shouted back.

Ms Boutros headed towards the main hall to check that the road safety assembly was wrapping up. She had tried this a minute ago, but had suddenly remembered she'd left an important . . . thing in the staff room and had turned back.

This time, as she neared the hall, she realised she had forgotten . . . something else. She wasn't sure what, but she needed to go back and get it. She turned on her heel and hurried towards her form room this time.

Bear and Troy exchanged a look.

BEAR
How much longer, Mulaki? We can't hold the Head off much longer.

MULAKI
Getting there.

In the main hall Mulaki had now joined Opie on stage, and was sweeping her mind-reading powers across the room, checking how well everyone's bubble techniques were working.

"Over there," she said, waving at a group of students to the left of the hall. "They're doing really well."

The students beamed smugly.

"Keep concentrating!" Opie warned. "Anything might be happening at the zoo. There could be confusion and running and screaming." She hoped she was exaggerating. "And you need to be able to keep that bubble inflated. It's the only thing that will keep you safe, okay?"

"Getting better over here," Mulaki said waving her hand towards another group. "This group is mainly good too; just one or two I can read easily. You have to concentrate, guys."

TROY

Opie, wrap it up, the Head is coming and we can't stop her this time. She's no idiot, she's written GO TO HALL on her hand and is walking with it held up in front of her face.

"Right, that's it, please go home and practice . . . road safety and pavement politeness," said Mulaki, diving for Xu's high-visibility yellow jacket and putting it on over her jacket as Ms Boutros entered the hall.

MULAKI

Please applaud now.

The school obediently broke into a round of applause. Opie joined in, flushed with triumph. That was the biggest group of people she had ever spoken in front of and it felt like . . . a success?

They would only know on Monday at the zoo.

Guess which one is me.

Good luck, I'm a master of disguise – oh.

Yeah. That is me.

You got lucky.

CHAPTER TWENTY-FIVE

OPIE SAT IN HER ROOM, WRITING AND REWRITING A note to Cillian. Malcolm was right, she'd done a terrible thing. She wanted Cillian to know how sorry she was.

Dear Cillian,

I hope you're okay. I had chicken pox once and got a scab up my nose, so I think I have an idea of how you're feeling. My mum ran peppermint teabags under the cold tap and placed them on the sores and it turned me green in patches but was soothing.

I'm sorry, ~~I think~~ I know it was my fault what happened to you and I take full responsibility.

~~Love~~

~~Regards~~

From Opie

Cillian didn't have to forgive her. But if he was going to come to the zoo on Monday, she HAD to teach him the bubble technique. That was the least she owed him.

She finished her note and turned to a portly wood pigeon perched on the edge of her desk. She tied the note to its leg.

"He's snarky," she warned. "But he has good reason to be," she added, being fair. "Ignore him if he snaps at you. Just give him the note."

The wood pigeon stamped his feet, adjusting to the weight of the paper on his leg before he was happy to spread its wings and fly off to Cillian's house.

About ten minutes later the wood pigeon fluttered back on to Opie's window sill, highly indignant.

WOOD PIGEON
He chucked me out of the window!

OPIE
I'm sorry!

WOOD PIGEON
Horrible little oik.
I was so shocked for a moment I forgot I could fly!

OPIE
You did remember?

WOOD PIGEON
Just before I hit the ground.

OPIE
Thank goodness.

Opie stood the wood pigeon on a plastic bag on her desk while she sprayed him with a little water spritzer. She apologetically stroked and rearranged his ruffled feathers.

WOOD PIGEON
How does the back of my head look?

Honestly? Small and grey, was Opie's first thought. Good thing she could read animal minds but they couldn't read hers.

OPIE
Majestic, simply majestic.

The wood pigeon made a bubbling cooing noise of pleasure.

WOOD PIGEON

Thought so.

The wood pigeon flatly refused to take another note, so Opie had to find another bird.

Unfortunately only one answered her call for help.

Then this girl, right, she was waving a sandwich around, cheese and pickle, and I thought *MINE*. So I grabbed it. But THEN I saw a dog with a biscuit and I wanted that too so I snatched it outta his mouth like HOOMMFF.

I legged it, girl AND dog chasing me. Ran right across a road, didn't even look. It was SO MUCH FUN.

CHAPTER TWENTY-SIX

FEELING UNCERTAIN, **O**PIE TIED HER SECOND NOTE TO the seagull's leg.

SEAGULL
What's that?

He prodded a lamp on her bedside table. It fell and smashed.

SEAGULL
Wicked. It broke.

Cillian had ignored Opie's texts *and* he'd ignored the wood pigeon. Well, he couldn't ignore a ruddy big seagull stomping around his bedroom. For his mum's sake, Opie hoped the seagull wouldn't do too much damage. But this was a risk she had to take.

There was a scuffling noise behind her as the seagull started a fight with a pile of books. Opie stared out of the window one last time, hoping to see a less feisty bird. No luck. With a sigh, she tied her note securely to the seagull's leg. It would need to survive any fights the gull got tangled up in during the journey.

Dear Cillian,

I know you're angry but I want to show you something that will help you stay safe at the zoo on Monday. I won't chat to you, I'll just show you what it is.
It's really important.
(Sorry about the seagull, I couldn't find a calmer bird.)

From ~~Opie~~
Dopey

Opie carried the seagull to the window.

SEAGULL
Oi! Gerroff me! You wanna fight?

OPIE
I'm helping you! Right, that house, there.
Can you see it?
Please stop pecking that.

SEAGULL
I peck what I want.

OPIE
Well done, you've broken it now.

SEAGULL
Wicked.

OPIE
There's a window with dinosaur stickers
on, can you fly in there?

SEAGULL
I can.

OPIE
Thank you!

SEAGULL
But WILL I?
Who knows.

Opie gently dropped the bird out of the window and watched it fly in big circles overhead, making rude noises at her.

OPIE
Please.

Eventually the bird stopped messing about and headed to Cillian's house.

Opie went back to her desk and looked at her notebook. Her crack team of animals wasn't coming along well.

- Malcolm (bad for my self-confidence, but fits in pocket)
- School rat (sings all the time but also fits in pocket)
- Pigeons (never listen)
- Budgies (dimmer than a broken lightbulb)
- Margot (unhelpful, moody, will eat team members 1-4, will not fit in pocket)
- Wood pigeon (annoyed at me, won't help)
- Seagull (LOL no)

She turned around at a noise behind her. A small snowy owl was pecking at the patterns on her duvet.

OWL

Did you want help with something?

OPIE

It's okay. I found a seagull.

The owl blinked at her, looking worried.

OWL

Good luck with that.

OPIE

Yeah ... I have some concerns.

The owl yawned.

OPIE

Sorry I woke you up.

OWL

S'all right. I'll get a bit more shut-eye, I think.

And it hopped up on to Opie's bed frame and tucked its head neatly beneath its wing.

Owl, Opie wrote in her notebook. She looked at the bird again. It was fast asleep. She added the note *nocturnal*. Not helpful for a daytime mission.

Opie carried on working, more quietly. Her bedroom was becoming a social club for any passing animal.

That was fine, until animals that fought or ate each other stopped by at the same time.

"Opie!" Violet called from downstairs.

Opie hurried down to see what her mother wanted.

Violet was on the phone, looking very confused. "It's Cillian's mum. She says there's a seagull in Cillian's bedroom? He says it's something to do with you? I said I didn't think so . . ."

Opie dashed to put her shoes on. "Tell them I'll come round now and sort it out," she said. "Oh, and Mum? Don't go in my room?"

Running, is it? Emergency.

  Yeah yeah, I'll help. Right behind you.
Just... give me ten minutes to find a snack.
I'll be no help to you if I'm hangry.

CHAPTER TWENTY-SEVEN

OPIE TURNED UP, OUT OF BREATH, ON CILLIAN'S doorstep. Liz let her in and ushered her upstairs, saying, "Please be safe, Opie. Should I call the RSPB?"

"No no no that's fine everything's fine!" yelped Opie, trying to sound calm.

This actually wasn't a bad thing to happen. At least this way she could talk to Cillian face to face. It would be hard to explain the bubble technique by note.

She reached the landing to find a livid Cillian, in a pair of Spider-Man pyjamas, clutching a pillow like a shield. She noticed he was holding her note, but thought it best not to mention it. He glared at her while she caught her breath at the top of the stairs.

"Your bites have gone down, they look much better," she gasped.

"Shut up."

"Did you do the peppermint teabag thing?"

"No," he said, but there were faint green squares on his face and arms.

Opie poked her head around Cillian's bedroom door and recoiled. Cillian's bedroom was chaos. The duvet was thrown aside, lamps were smashed and the lead to his Playstation was wrapped around the seagull's leg.

Opie backed out of the room. "Um," she said. "Is your bedroom usually a mess?"

His tone was icy. "No. I keep it really nice."

"Ah. So this is recent . . . bird damage . . ."

"Yes."

"I'll help you tidy it."

"You can tidy it by yourself!" he snapped.

Opie thought she'd rather face the seagull than Cillian right now so went back into the bedroom. The seagull was squaring up to his own reflection in the wardrobe mirror, making aggressive squawking noises.

OPIE
That's you.

SEAGULL
I'm me! This lad wants a fight, he's getting all up in my face.

Opie stood behind the gull, who stared in amazement at her reflection. He experimentally pecked the mirror. Then he pecked real Opie.

"Ow," said Opie.

SEAGULL
Don't like it. Want to go home.

Opie made soothing noises as she unwrapped the lead from the seagull's leg.

OPIE

Think about things you like.

Stolen sandwiches, shouting people, hooting cars . . .

She could feel the seagull relax, and he became quite docile, allowing her to pick him up and drop him gently out of the window. He flew away, yelling happily, looking for new trouble.

Opie set to work cleaning Cillian's bedroom. It helped her guilt to do something nice for him. She swept his broken lamps into the bin, untangled his Playstation and made his bed. She picked up some photos that had been knocked off his wall. They were of Jackson and Cillian, some from when they were small kids. She never realised . . . they'd been friends so long.

It was easy to see Cillian as a sarcastic, prickly person. She'd never considered how he felt about *her*: someone who was trying to take his best friend away from him. Stuck at home with a face that Jackson said was too 'gross' to look at, he must've felt gutted, imagining Opie and Jackson having fun and forgetting about him.

Opie was working so hard she didn't hear the door open. She realised that Cillian was behind her.

"You don't have to clean up," he said.

"I do. I sent a ruddy seagull into your bedroom," she said.

He gave a short laugh. "He was massive, Opie!" Opie noticed that, for once, he didn't call her Dopey. "What were you *thinking*?"

"I was thinking you could ignore a text but you couldn't ignore him," she said.

They both laughed and then stood a little awkwardly in silence.

"Did it poo anywhere?" Cillian said, breaking the silence.

"I don't think so. If he did, I haven't found it yet."

"I'll check my slippers."

Cillian started tidying his books while Opie used her T-shirt sleeve to wipe his mirror. It was covered in peck marks.

"Your note," he said. "What did you want to teach me?"

Opie had been wondering how to bring it up. "I think I can teach you how to protect yourself from mind control," she said in relief. "I want you to . . . I mean, best if you're safe, isn't it?"

"OK," he said. "Thanks for . . . you know. Thinking of me and whatever."

"Oh yeah, of course. Whatever," Opie said, concentrating very hard on cleaning the mirror and not making eye contact. She took a green and orange friendship bracelet out of her pocket and put it on his bedside table.

When she next looked around it had gone.

We're out!

We're out! Had a BALLER time.

Well, you hummed Christmas songs for
twenty days. In summer. But I am very
happy with my new look.

WELL happy.

I love your wings. I never realised there
were so many shades of brown, you're like
a tabby cat.

Cheers. I love it, love the
whole look. Flying's a bonus.

CHAPTER TWENTY-EIGHT

ACROSS TOWN, TWENTY-FIVE WELL-DRESSED MEN AND women were standing on the penthouse floor of a tall office block. They were staring out of the floor-to-ceiling windows on one side of the room. There was the heavy silence you got with a bunch of telepaths, as everyone communicated solely via thoughts.

Max Inkelaar was sitting in an armchair while they stood. He liked doing that, to remind them of his importance.

Hugo Varling, as Max's boss, was keen to prove he was the *most* important, so he'd gone one step further and was having a bath. He kept the bathroom door open so he could yell at them.

"Don't even think you're getting overtime for this

job!" He snapped, placing a cucumber slice over each eye.

The small lilac-haired woman who'd tried to cause chaos at Opie's school was there. Her name was Zienna. She was staring out of the window, fiddling with her nose ring. She tapped on the glass and looked down at people, tiny as grains of rice scattered on the streets below.

ZIENNA
This window is in the way.

MAX
That's rather the point.

No one wanted to say, *Huh? I don't get it*, so the silence in the room got even heavier. The telepaths hid their confusion and tried to look intelligent. A couple of them rubbed their chins because that always makes you look clever.

Max wasn't fooled. He sighed at the stupidity of his team.

MAX

I need you to practise distance and focus.

There was a splashing noise in the bathroom.

"Chop chop!" Hugo Varling shouted. "Get started! What are they not understanding? I want to hear cars screaming and chaos thirteen floors down. Get on it!"

"Why, what's the point?" Zienna asked. "Just to cause damage?"

There was the squeak of a rubber duck squeezed hard.

"Because your boss told you to. That's an excellent reason," Varling said icily.

Half of the telepaths turned to the window, looking resigned, ready to get started. The other half, including Zienna, did not. There was a busy road and thousands of people hurrying around down there. If they provoked random fights, people could be badly hurt.

ZIENNA

This isn't right.

"Are they arguing?" Hugo drawled lazily from the bathroom.

"Not for long," Max assured his boss.

MAX

It is right, Zienna. Because we pay you for your time and skills.

You use the money to help your mother and you do as we tell you or the money dries up.

It's very simple. Get to it.

Zienna jumped at the faint sound of a car crash, many storeys below.

MAX

Well done, Damon.

A tubby man in his forties smirked at Max. He caught Zienna's eye and looked awkward.

DAMON

It was just an ice-cream van.

Sprinkles everywhere but no one's hurt.

ZIENNA
That man's got a Flake up his nose.

DAMON
It'll melt.

MAX
<u>Hurt</u> someone next time.

Damon's smirk faltered.

"I don't hear smashes, sirens and screams!" Hugo bawled from the bath. "Smashes, sirens and screams! Smashes, sirens and screams!"

He started to chant his new disgusting motto, splashing the bathwater in rhythm.

I'm trying not to panic but I am definitely
lost.

    I'm on someone's face. I think they're
sleeping.

    Uh oh. They're waking up. I hope they
don't mind me being here.

CHAPTER TWENTY-NINE

AS WITH ALL SCARY DAYS, MONDAY HEADED TOWARDS Opie with terrifying speed.

Ms Boutros had asked them all to dress neatly. Opie had two thoughts as she got ready in her smartest dungarees for the zoo. One: it didn't matter how well-dressed they were when two hundred students were punching lumps out of each other and giraffes were screaming in horror. And two, she sighed as she packed her Saint Francis of Assisi backpack: this might be the last time she wore this bag if today went badly and Varling's plans came to pass.

Opie was surprised by how much she had grown to love her school. At the beginning of term she'd been shy and had no friends. Now she had two (maybe one and a half), and since teaching the school the bubble technique she was on nodding terms with everyone.

At least she'd still see them . . . in the new Saint Francis of Assisi warehouse.

Her biggest worry was Jackson.

Cillian had picked up the bubble technique quite easily. She'd taken him to the local cinema to bother Troy who, in between selling tickets, had tried and failed to read Cillian's mind. He'd sent them on their way with congratulations and a box of popcorn. Jackson was a different matter. He couldn't concentrate, or wouldn't. He said it would be fine, he'd do it on the day, but Opie was still trying to persuade him this wasn't school, he couldn't coast through on cheek and charm. She didn't think he believed her.

Cillian had promised to stick close to Jackson as Opie would be too busy to keep an eye on him.

Opie stared out of her window, smoothing down her shirt. She used to love the sunshine, until Mulaki told her that Varling incited riots in summer because people were more likely to get violent in the heat. She'd googled that and found Mulaki was right. There weren't many photos of rioting people in woolly hats and gloves. Fighting in knitwear probably felt like a massage.

Violet was taking Opie, Jackson and Cillian to Regent's Park where she'd sunbathe and wait for them. "Unless you want me to traipse around the zoo in the heat?" she'd offered, unwillingly.

"No no," Opie said. "Stay in the park, enjoy the sun."

"Worried I'll embarrass you?" her mum had twinkled at her.

Worried we're all going to be horribly wounded, Opie thought, faking a smile.

At least Harvey was filming, so he'd be safe. Whether Dr Ahmed was safe was another matter. Opie was still waiting for the script for the next episode.

There was a knock at the front door and she saw the outlines of Jackson and Cillian through the wavy glass.

"Hey," she said, her voice shaky.

"I know," said Cillian, looking as anxious as she felt.

"Do you know," chirped Jackson, "I've never actually been to the zoo?"

Opie was glad Cillian was there. Jackson was oblivious to worry and it made people around him worry twice as much.

The four of them headed towards the train station, with Jackson, Cillian and Opie loitering behind Violet so that they could talk.

"Have you been practising the bubble thing?" Opie asked Jackson quietly.

"Yes," said Jackson.

"Thank goodness."

"But it was boring so I stopped."

"Argh, *Jackson*."

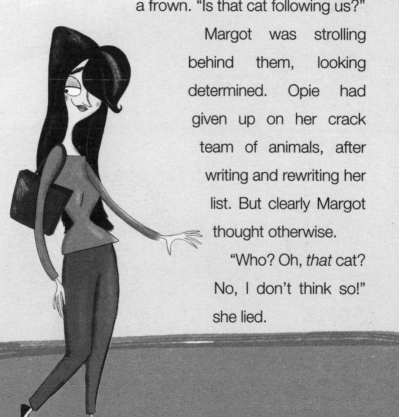

"Opie?" Violet said, looking back with a frown. "Is that cat following us?"

Margot was strolling behind them, looking determined. Opie had given up on her crack team of animals, after writing and rewriting her list. But clearly Margot thought otherwise.

"Who? Oh, *that* cat? No, I don't think so!" she lied.

OPIE
What are you doing?

MARGOT
Helping.

"Helping how?" Opie was so surprised, she spoke that instead of thinking it.

"Is that our secret weapon?" Cillian asked. "An overweight cat?"

Margot stopped dead in her tracks.

MARGOT
I am not overweight. I am Maine Coon on my mother's side.

I will not be body shamed by a boy with a body like a twig.

OPIE
I know! You're beautiful, he doesn't mean it.

MARGOT

I am a natural born leader.

I am coming to lead this Resistance.

And I've never been to the zoo.

I want to meet a lion and swap haircare tips.

Opie shrugged at Cillian and Jackson, and hoped that Violet would forget about the large tabby cat following them into Central London.

But that was impossible. The moment the cat hopped on the train, people started taking photos of her. Margot played up horribly to the attention, winding her body around the central pole and pulling winsome poses.

"Aw," said Violet. "The puddy cat *is* coming with us!"

MARGOT

I won't even dignify that with a response.

There is more to me than just the long
neck you know.

But, yes, fine. I'll be your lookout.

CHAPTER THIRTY

OPIE BREATHED A SIGH OF RELIEF. **T**HE GIRAFFE WOULD be helpful for spotting potential problems. She'd forgotten how big the zoo was. She would have to run fast to cover the ground.

It was ten-thirty, and there was already a twitchy, nervous feeling in the air. Hugo Varling had met them all at the entrance to the zoo and made a speech about 'Giving Back To The Community' and other such lies about himself. The Saint Francis of Assisi students had listened with their arms folded and sarcastic looks on their faces.

Varling had brought photographers, who bounced around, squatting and lunging on their tiptoes to catch their boss from every flattering angle. But no matter how many times they tried, they couldn't get a single shot of a school pupil looking pleased. Varling would probably spin that on his website as 'ungrateful students descend into brawling chaos' if the day went as badly as Opie feared.

No. She shook herself. She would think positively. She had told her schoolmates what to expect, so they were braced to defend themselves.

Once in the zoo, they split into five groups: A, B, C, D and Blue, because Monsieur Lunarca hadn't listened properly when Ms Boutros had outlined the plan. Always the maverick, he'd gone through the gift shop first and Opie could see his big hippo hat bobbing around in the crowd.

Opie was in Group C, while Cillian and Jackson were in Group A. In normal circumstances, she'd have been jealous. But she had bigger problems today.

Ms Boutros was so grateful to the nice road safety group, who had not only taken a school assembly for her, but had also offered to help with the zoo trip. Group C walked with their 'chaperone' Mulaki. As they passed the aquarium, Opie heard tiny screaming. She darted inside. Had Varling started already? He had disappeared as soon as he'd made his speech, and she'd caught a glimpse of him leaving the zoo.

FISHES
Help! Banging banging! LOUD!

"Oi!" shouted Opie, surprising herself with the volume of her voice. "Don't bang on the glass. Read the sign!"

A group of tourists froze, their palms on the glass, and looked embarrassed. A starfish peeled itself off the side of the glass and floated away, looking dizzy.

STARFISH
Bleurgh. Thanks.
So queasy.

Opie ducked back into the hot sunshine. She blinked, temporarily blinded. She had been so sure the mayhem was about to begin.

She was reassured to see The Resistance striding towards her. They looked like proper superheroes.

Xu had a new cape on, Troy was out of his cinema uniform and Bear had even ironed his T-shirt, which was yellow and said *Everything Is Going To Be OK.* Opie hoped Bear's T-shirt was right. She looked down at her dungarees. Maybe she should get some glittery boots?

She was distracted by a mob forming around the lion enclosure. She and Bear exchanged a look and ran over. But it turned out that the tourists were captivated by Margot lolling in a tree, chatting to a lion about getting tangles out of long fur and agreeing the best technique was to get a human servant to do it.

Mulaki started directing members of The Resistance into place. "I'm sticking with this group. Troy, stay in the sloth area as there are no protective bars. I want you all to stick close to the enclosures where someone could jump in."

Opie felt ill. Of course that's what Varling would make someone do.

"And Bear," Mulaki added, "stay near the polar bears and keep an eye on the hippos."

"Hippos are covered," said Opie. "I have the giraffes on lookout and they're right next door. But are you sure we should split up? Should we have walkie talkies or . . ."

"Oh bless," said Xu patronisingly.

"Opie, we can all . . ." Mulaki pointed between all their heads.

Opie blushed. "Oh right, of course."

"Fling the cat in the air if you need help," said Xu.

MARGOT

Try it. I dare you.

"Good luck Opie," Mulaki said. "You're going to be great."

Mulaki gave a reassuring thumbs up to Opie, who did them back, completely unaware of the message Mulaki was sending to everyone else.

MULAKI

Do not let her get hurt.

If it looks like it's going down, the closest person grabs her and the boys and runs them to her mother in the park.

"Mulaki? Why is everyone nodding at you?" Opie asked.

The Resistance immediately looked at their feet or the sky.

Mulaki sighed. "Because they're blithering idiots. All right, let's do this thing!"

Despite herself, Opie felt a swelling of excitement. She was going into battle for her school.

I'm not unreasonable. I don't need to eat a
whole person.

Half. Just half a person.

C'mon.

CHAPTER THIRTY-ONE

*N*o! Opie told the hippo. *Stop nagging. And you* *can't eat half a person. It's not like the half left* *behind will lead a full and happy life, is it?*

The zoo was a very noisy place in Opie's head. She hadn't really considered how many different animals would be chatting while she tried to stop her school from rioting. She was getting a headache.

She had imagined a zoo full of exotic animals would have a lot of accents. But most of the zoo animals were born in captivity, so it was mainly London accents. It sounded like the background chat on a bus.

Then there were the human voices too. Bear was with Group A, and kept up a running commentary in Opie's head. Opie saw Cillian look at Bear and nod occasionally, like Bear was talking to him.

BEAR
Nothing so far.
Where are Varling's guys?

Another voice popped into Opie's mind.

MARGOT
We must have code names.

OPIE
There you are! Where are you?

MARGOT
I'm leading from the front.
I have decided my code name is Michelle Obama.

OPIE
OK, fine. But can you tell me where you are?
Margot?
Margot?
... Michelle Obama?

MARGOT
Yes hello.

OPIE
Why don't you answer me?

MARGOT
Because I did not think the idea of code
names was that complicated.

On the other side of the zoo, Mulaki skim-read
through the minds of the crowd, looking for trouble. A
sudden scream made her jump, but it was just a baby.
She and Troy made gritted-teeth smiles at each other,
sharing the tension.

TROY
Anything?

MULAKI
Hundreds of kids wishing they were at home
on their XBox. You?

TROY
Kelly fancies a boy called Conrad. But Conrad fancies Siobhan.
That's the gossip from Group B.

MULAKI
Conrad?

TROY
In Group Blue.
Dreamboat, apparently. And he really listens.

A group of Saint Francis kids were queuing to get into the After Dark building – a scruffy, gangly boy behind a pristine student with neatly combed hair. The pristine boy made a noise of annoyance.

"Do you want to back off a bit?" he said to the scruffy kid. "You're breathing on the back of my head, I can feel it."

"What?"

"Give me some room. Stop crowding me, you weirdo."

"I'm crowding you? In a CROWD? If you don't like it, stay home."

The neat boy suddenly shoved the scruffy kid, who stumbled back into a group of people behind him, knocking a couple of small children to the ground. One started to cry. One of Varling's photographers slunk forward, fiddling with his camera.

Ms Boutros ran towards the fight, but several pupils got there first.

"Bubble! Bubble!" they hissed at the fighting kids, who instantly started concentrating. After a moment, they released their grip on each other's clothes.

"Sorry," the scruffy boy whispered. "I *was* standing too close."

Varling's photographer turned away, looking annoyed. He hadn't got any of the photos he wanted.

Opie hadn't realised she'd been holding her breath. It was horrifying to see how quickly a fight could escalate. The zoo was busy as usual, so any fights were likely to spill over into the general public. And there were lots of small children around, kids too young to be in school. The risk of a toddler getting trampled was worryingly high.

Opie was trying her best to 'create moments of wonder', like Mulaki had said. But she was struggling.

OPIE
Murmuration, it's a thing.

PIGEON #400
Nah mate. You're thinking of Monument.

OPIE
I'm not.

PIGEON #32
Monument! You are, it's by Bank. Tube station.

PIGEON #11
You wanna get there now, you hop on the bus, the stop's just outside Regent's Park.

OPIE

A murmuration is where you all swoop through the air, as one. Starlings do it, but I can't find any starlings. Could you give it a try?

Pigeon #45 made a whistling noise as he sucked air through his beak.

PIGEON #45

So we're what, Plan B? The silver medal? Not great for the old ego, mate.

OPIE

Sorry. But I'm sure you'd do a great job. You need to swoop and soar at the same time, I'll give you commands –

PIGEON #400

Commands?

OPIE
Requests. It'll be beautiful and everyone will admire you and I'd be really grateful.

PIGEON #678
And what's the pay like?

OPIE
I have three oat snack bars.

PIGEON #19
That's gonna get you about ten of us, I reckon, unless any young birds wanna do it for free for a bit of work experience?

YOUNG PIGEON
I will! But I can't fly very well.

Margot was listening to this from the tiger enclosure, laughing until she was weak.

OPIE
Michelle Obama, you are not helping!

MARGOT
I'm not <u>trying</u> to help.

Opie gave up and went back to patrolling the zoo, looking for trouble. Varling's photographer moved with her, doing the same thing.

The problem was that they couldn't see any of Varling's telepaths, so they couldn't predict where fights would start.

Mulaki threw a thought to Bear, Troy and Xu.

MULAKI
Where is Varling? I have a nasty feeling he's trying something new.

BEAR
Don't say that. His old nonsense is bad enough.

Opie watched her four new friends pacing around alongside the school kids. They looked more anxious than she had ever seen them. For the first time, Opie understood how impossible this was. It was like watching people chuck lit matches at a pool of petrol, while The Resistance ran around with tiny water pistols, putting out fires.

And one person chatting uselessly to a pigeon, she thought with a sigh. There was that feeling of inadequacy Malcolm talked about.

Still, if her job was to be 'the fluff', best get on with it.

"Aaaaah!"

Troy, Bear, Xu and Mulaki stopped their anxious conversation as they suddenly felt a rush of pleasure and joy from people near the llama enclosure.

They hurried over to see three llamas balancing on top of each other.

"I don't know what they're doing!" the zoo keeper exclaimed, laughing. "We never taught them that!"

People were enchanted. Tourists were getting out their phones to film the adorable sight. Parents were lifting little kids up to see better. Mulaki looked at Opie, who was concentrating hard.

LLAMA

Why are we doing this?

OPIE

Very complicated reasons.

But you are doing me such a favour and I appreciate it.

LLAMA

No worries mate.

Might get down now though. This one's hooves aren't comfy on my back.

BABY LLAMA

Whinge whinge whinge.

There was a laugh from the crowd as the llamas sprang apart, sending the baby llama on top flying into a pile of straw.

XU

Well done, Opie.

Opie kept walking around the zoo, looking left and right, tense and alert for the slightest hint of trouble.

OPIE
You OK, Michelle Obama?

MARGOT
Working hard.

Opie glanced at the roof of the cafe, where all she could see of Margot was her lazily flicking tail.

MARGOT
Mentally rather than physically...

Bear suddenly ran past Opie towards Jackson, who had a look on his face that Opie had never seen before. She saw him shake his head groggily. He took his phone out of his pocket, but then stared at it as if he couldn't remember what it was.

Jackson suddenly wheeled around and marched away from Group A, heading towards the hippo enclosure. Cillian pulled on his arm, frantically whispering, "Bubble bubble bubble!" But it was useless.

Jackson was in the grip of a powerful mind control.

On the edge of Regent's Park, on the balcony of a luxurious flat, Hugo Varling drank a refreshing cup of tea and stared at an iPad. He was surrounded by all his telepaths, who were crammed uncomfortably close together. Damon's nose was buried in the back of Zienna's head . He was discreetly trying to spit lilac hairs out of his mouth.

"Focus on the catalysts, Max," Hugo said without looking up from his iPad. "A few kids going berserk – that's all it takes."

"Yes," said Max, a little testily. "We *have* discussed this several times before."

"Look at that tall kid. Put three on him."

Max Inkelaar rolled his eyes without Hugo seeing. "I have. Can't you see he's heading for the hippos?"

Max was an experienced telepath. He did not need

an annoying boss telling him what to do. Not that he'd say that. It was risky to even think it. He glanced at the telepaths on the balcony with him, but they all kept their faces smooth. It was not sensible to read the boss's thoughts. Especially when he was in such a bad mood.

The telepaths were busy anyway, all targeting different Saint Francis of Assisi students. Their powers were weaker at a distance, but they'd been practising. The photographers only needed a couple of seconds of fighting or vandalism to get their photos and they'd be all over the internet by this evening, looking far worse than the reality.

Back in the zoo, Opie darted through crowds of people, trying to reach Jackson. To her horror he had already climbed over the railings meant to keep visitors out of the hippopotamus enclosure, scaling them easily with his long legs.

Now he was inching out over a narrow walkway that was just two poles lashed together. It wasn't something a person was ever meant to walk on. Members of the public gathered around the edge of the enclosure and gasped at the danger Jackson was in. Some got out their phones and started filming.

Beneath him, the hippos gathered, licking their lips.

HIPPO
I'll just eat half.

OPIE
You won't eat ANY.

HIPPO
Watch me.

Opie realised she was not going to be able to reason with the hippos. So she scrambled over the railings and followed Jackson on to the walkway, wobbling dangerously.

"Opie!" Xu shouted.

The surprise made Opie stumble and nearly fall. She crouched on the poles and swayed over the enclosure. She could see the dark brown water below and the ripples of a hippo waiting just below the surface.

OPIE
Oh my god, not helping.

XU
Sorry.

Opie gripped the walkway with shaking hands and pushed herself up again. To her horror, Jackson had reached the end. Now there was nowhere to go but into the pool teaming with hippos.

Opie looked around helplessly. She was gutted to see all of Varling's photographers gathered around the edge of the enclosure, some filming, some taking photos. But she also saw a lot of familiar faces. Saint Francis of Assisi students had pushed their way to the front of the crowd and were watching the danger, hands over their mouths. Some were urging Jackson to do the balloon technique – but it was too late.

There seemed to be only one way Jackson and Opie were getting off this walkway – a fall, a splash and a crunch.

Opie pictured the zoo map, trying to find any animal who would help. They were all stuck in their own enclosures and unable to get out. And the ones that could get out couldn't really help.

WALLABY
Oi. I'm stronger than I look.

OPIE
No offence.

She couldn't call any birds for help; what could they do? There was no bird that could lift her or Jackson out of danger. But she hadn't come this far to leave him.

A blur of brown fur shot past her. Margot trotted along the railing, easily keeping her balance. She reached Jackson and started climbing his tall frame. Opie winced. She'd been climbed by Margot before, and all that wriggling weight hanging off sharp claws was not a pleasant experience.

But Jackson, his brain full of telepathic thoughts telling him to jump, barely even noticed.

"Arms out, Jackson!" she heard Ms Mollo shout from the sidelines.

Jackson showed no sign that he had heard, but Opie followed Ms Mollo's advice. It definitely helped her to balance better. But it would only take one strong gust of wind to overbalance her into the hippopotamus pool.

She glanced down again. The bulk of a huge hippo broached the surface of the water, his tiny ears and broad back first, then his nose and eyes. His eyes were staring up at her, unblinking. He opened his mouth slightly, waiting.

GIRAFFE

Excuse me, tiny little girl?

Just to let you know.

There are two people about to fall in the hippo pool.

OPIE
Thank you. Great lookout work.

GIRAFFE
I know, right?

Jackson stood frozen at the end of the walkway. Opie had just enough time to reach him. She hoped he was fighting the voices in his head. She knew what they would be saying.

JUMP.

She reached Jackson and gently grabbed a handful of his polo shirt at the back, hoping to keep hold of him if he tried it. They both stood there, wobbling gently on legs like jelly.

MARGOT
Don't die, Opie . . .

OPIE
Trying not to.

MARGOT

... cos you're my lift home.

Margot clambered on to Jackson's shoulders, almost making him lose his balance.

"Margot, can you not?" snapped Opie.

MARGOT

If we get eaten by hippos those will be the last words you ever say to me.

You will feel AWFUL.

OPIE

I think I'll cope. I won't have long to dwell on it.

Up on the balcony on the edge of Regent's Park, Varling was out of his seat and watching through binoculars, chuckling gently to himself.

"Is that the animal mind-reader?" he asked. Max nodded.

"An *animal* mind-reader?" Damon scoffed. "She

might be good in a circus . . ." But he fell silent under Varling's withering gaze.

"What animal are you scared of, Damon?" Varling asked silkily. "Everyone's scared of something."

"Spiders," Damon admitted.

"Imagine that girl heading towards you with a hundred tarantulas who do whatever she tells them to."

Damon imagined it.Varling put his hands together, fingertip to fingertip, and enjoyed how unhappy Damon looked. Max hated how much his boss enjoyed other people's misery.

"So," said Varling. "She's playing with cats right now. When she joins our side, we're going to give her her wolves, tigers, bears . . . Think of any animal that scares you." He turned to his team. "Then imagine a pack of them, hunting *you*, controlled by *her*."

Unaware that she was being discussed like a dangerous weapon, Opie kept a tight hold of Jackson's polo shirt and murmured comforting things that she didn't believe.

Out of the corner of her eye, she saw Mulaki.

Panting slightly from her sprint across the zoo, Mulaki was now standing across from Jackson. Staring at him intently, she worked on blasting the three telepaths clean out of his mind with a wave of positive thoughts.

Back on the balcony, Max watched the faces of the three telepaths targeting Jackson. As one, they staggered back, wincing with pain.

"What's happening?" Hugo Varling demanded.

"Mulaki, of course," said Max shortly.

"God damn it," Varling spat, tossing his iPad to the floor in a temper. "I would swap all of you for her."

Jackson came to his senses, terrified to find himself on a flimsy pole overhanging a pool of hippos.

"That you, Opie?" he said, reaching carefully behind him to hold the hand clutching his shirt.

"Yeah," said Opie. "I'm here."

"I'm so sorry! I did the balloon thing, I promise!"

"It's not your fault. We're all doing our best," Opie said, talking to herself as much as to him.

"Don't move!" a zoo keeper shouted.

"I mean . . ." Jackson gestured gently as if to say, 'Where on earth would we go?'

"Don't make me laugh, Jackson," Opie said, grinning despite herself.

A second later, she got the shock of her life. Someone grabbed the back of *her* shirt, just like she had done to Jackson. She jumped and wobbled.

The shocks continued.

"Careful," Cillian said.

Opie turned her head, and saw a line of Saint Francis students behind her and Jackson on the walkway. They had edged out, hanging on tightly to each other, forming a human chain. The poles were bowing slightly under their weight.

It was the bravest thing Opie had ever seen.

MULAKI

Well done everyone.

Now, you're going to edge back, one step at a time.

I'll count you down so you all step at the same time and no one jostles anyone, OK?

Mulaki started counting and the students moved in time together, tiny step by tiny step. Monsieur Lunarca and Ms Boutros were there to help everyone back over the rail to safety, though Monsieur Lunarca struggled with the bigger students. The plan worked perfectly – until Margot got impatient and started walking over everyone's head and shoulders to get off the walkway quicker.

This is why no one has cat sidekicks, Opie thought.

She inched behind the line of students, keeping a tight hold of Jackson. He had been standing on the narrow walkway for longer than anyone, and she could tell his legs had become stiff and clumsy.

"Look at the pigeons! What are they doing?" cried a man with a booming voice.

"The pigeons are possessed!" a girl shrieked dramatically.

Now the pigeons want to murmurate? So unhelpful, Opie thought. "Don't look up, guys, don't lose your balance!" she called out to the wobbly line of students.

All around them were flashes of sharp white light.

"Is that lightning?" a kid asked further up the line.

"Photographers," Opie said, shortly.

The day had descended into chaos and all their plans had failed. Opie's nose stung with unshed tears as she finally clambered back over the rail, making sure Jackson followed her safely. They had all made it back in one piece (and not one big flat piece) but she still felt bitterly disappointed.

She wasn't the only one.

HIPPO
Aw. Not fair.

Unruly pupils terrorise hippos. Opie could imagine the headlines now. *Shut this school down, the students are a menace*.

From the look on Mulaki's face, she felt the same as Opie. But she folded Opie into her arms for a quick tight hug.

MULAKI
You did so well. Come on, let's get everyone home.

Monsieur Lunarca and Ms Boutros were combining the groups, taking two each to get them all back to the coach quickly. The students were shaken and quiet, all obediently doing as they were told, so it was quick work for the teachers to get them out of the zoo and away from the photographers. In the confusion, neither teacher noticed that Opie, Jackson and Cillian had hung back.

Opie glanced around.

OPIE
Michelle Obama?

"Ooof!"

Margot landed in Opie's arms, knocking the wind out of her lungs.

MARGOT
Fun fact. My weight is mainly muscle.

OPIE
Sure, whatever.

Opie clutched Margot tightly. People were now streaming out of the zoo, maybe worrying that someone else was about to try and fling themselves in with the hippos.

OPIE
Here, get in my bag.

Margot clambered into Opie's schoolbag. Opie could hear her thoughts, tutting about the three smashed-up Oaty bars in there.

MARGOT
Look at this.
Oats all over my fur.
If it rains I'll turn into a CAKE.

As Jackson, Cillian and Opie left the zoo, Opie paused. She took the time to thank the animals who had tried to help her. Then they headed towards the park to find Violet, walking in a sad silence.

Cillian seemed to know how she was feeling. "You tried," he told her.

Opie nodded, wiping her eyes and nose.

"Remember Dopey, you're only ten," he said kindly. "And your skill is a bit rubbish. Good thing I was there to rescue you both."

The Resistance hung back to check that everyone had left the zoo safely. Xu took a piece of chalk out of his pocket and drew a big, bold, defiant shape on the ground. He hoped Varling would see it.

CHAPTER THIRTY-TWO

"**H**EROIC KIDS RESCUE CLASSMATE," OPIE READ OFF Cillian's phone. "*See the moment youngsters work together to save a life. You won't believe what happens next.* Oh look Cillian, you can really see your face in this one!"

They had travelled home in desperately low spirits, convinced that Varling's plan had succeeded and The Resistance had failed. And for the first half hour of the journey, they had been reading terrible articles on Varling's website called things like "*Nightmare kids terrorise zoo*".

But then other websites took the same video and started writing articles about students working together and rescuing Jackson. It all depended how you chose to see the footage. And most of the articles were positive. They were calling Saint Francis students heroes! They were also calling Jackson an idiot.

Jackson didn't mind. He looked extremely handsome in the videos and photographs and he was happy with that.

By the time they reached their train station, the three friends were jubilant. Jackson and Cillian ran off home to fetch their bikes and then cycled over to Opie's house, balancing one of Cillian's old bikes between them for Opie to use.

"Time to celebrate our victorious day!" Cillian cried, clambering to the top of a hill with his legs either side of his bike. "Come on, it'll be FUN!"

"Just because you say something is fun, doesn't make it so," complained Opie, who was following behind on Cillian's old bike with Jackson.

"Yes but it IS!" Cillian said, bouncing up and down on his pedals. "I've built jumps there, there and there." He pointed them out. "You've got to zigzag between them." For some reason, he had seen this dangerously steep hill and thought it needed extra peril and more risk of injury.

"OK OK," said Opie, resigning herself to an inevitable broken leg. She waddled awkwardly on the bike to the top of Cillian's Stupid Hill of Unnecessary Danger (she had given it that name) and gulped at how steep it was.

At the bottom of the hill, sunning herself on a bench, was Margot, who Opie was starting to consider a sidekick. A terrible one, sure. But crack teams don't assemble themselves overnight.

Opie had asked her parents if Margot could maybe come and stay at theirs sometimes and Harvey had said, "Of course! What a privilege, I've always dreamed of spending money feeding someone else's cat part-time."

Harvey hadn't mentioned whether Dr Ahmed was still stuck in a ditch with a broken leg. Opie really wanted to bin Max Inkelaar's business card, but told herself she would wait until Dr Ahmed got rescued or hopped to safety on his one good leg. It was important to have options.

"You go first, Opie," said Cillian, interrupting her thoughts.

"No way!" she yelped.

"Um yes?" he said like she was stupid. "Because the first person down the run has the easiest time of it because that's when the mud isn't so slippery. So I'm actually doing you a favour?"

"That's so nice of you, Cilly," Jackson said, sincerely.

Opie stared down the hill with some strong doubts about that. As her frenemy, Cillian had been more fren than enemy lately, but maybe he was reverting back to his old catty ways.

MARGOT
Don't say catty when you mean mean.

OPIE
Sorry.

MARGOT
Bigoted, innit.

Opie rolled the front wheel of her bike just over the lip of the hill, to get a better look at Cillian's ridiculous homemade jumps. But the front wheel kept moving, and then the back wheel followed and, with a squawk, Opie was suddenly rolling down the side of a steep hill, MUCH faster than she wanted.

Cillian exclaimed behind her, "Oh no! She's doing it!"

Which didn't fill her with confidence. But it was too late now. She had hit the first jump with a rattle from the bike and suddenly she was flying! A whoop of glee burst out of her, but was cut short with an "erk" noise as she landed and skidded towards the second jump.

"Be careful!" Cillian yelled, as if she had any control over it and this wasn't ALL his fault.

Opie bounced off the second jump and was flying again. This time she got cocky and took one hand off her handlebar to punch the air.

That was a mistake.

The bike hit the ground, and Opie only had one hand on the handlebar to control it. So the bike wobbled violently and before she knew it, she was sliding down the hill on her left side, still clinging on to the bike.

"Dopey, you stacked it!" crowed Cillian.

Opie's recent warm feelings towards him evaporated into a cloud of dust, grass and shredded skin. She slid over the third jump, which finally brought her to a stop. Then she crawled painfully down the rest of the hill to lie on the cool grass and count her remaining limbs.

Eyes closed, Opie wiggled her toes, fingers and nose. She was reassured to find that these were still attached and responding to instructions.

"Opie!" Jackson ran towards her and flung himself to his knees beside her. "Are you OK?"

She gave him a silent thumbs up.

Cillian arrived a second later. "Well, the main thing is, you made that look elegant. Oh hello."

"What?" Opie opened her eyes and found that her mum had joined Jackson and Cillian to stare down at her.

"Oh kids, I'm so sorry," said Violet. She was holding her phone. "I thought you should know, the parents just got an email asking them to come to an emergency meeting to discuss the future of your school tomorrow. It doesn't sound good."

"What? But we're heroes!" cried Cillian.

"I know, sweets. It's not fair," said Violet. "We'll see what they say in the meeting. There's a businessman coming along too, let me find his name . . . maybe he'll offer some help?"

"Is it Varling?" said Opie dully.

"Yes, that's it!" said Violet. "So, don't despair. Maybe he'll help."

Opie knew her mum meant well. But if ever there was a time to despair, it was now.

Margot ran over and rubbed her body against

ACKNOWLEDGEMENTS

Thanks as always to my wonderful agent Hellie Ogden, as well as Kirsty Gordon, Ma'suma Amiri and Claire Conrad at Janklow and Nesbit. Thank you to my editor Liz Bankes who loved Opie, even at the early stages when I was playing fast and loose with logic! I didn't get a chance to meet everyone at Egmont and Harper Collins properly thanks to Covid, but I appreciate you all from a safe distance! Thanks to Lucy Courtenay, Becky Peacock, Olivia Adams, Ryan Hammond, Laura Bird, Beth Chaplin-Dewey and Siobhan McDermott.

Huge thanks to Fay Austin, who brought Opie to life, alongside a horde of animal characters. You're brilliant and I love every one of them.

Lots of love and thanks to my friends who kept me sane and happy through lockdown, I hope I did the same for you. (I totally did, what a sweetheart.)

This book is inspired by the real Margot von Catton, my huge and surly Maine Coon. Thanks to my long-suffering mum and dad who adopted Margot when she grew bored of me and started flipping my television over for fun. And thanks to my brother Michael for being a rock this year. I don't even mind that the cat loves you more than me.

BOOK TWO

ANIMAL QUIZ

Where is your favourite place to sleep?

A. Somewhere inconvenient to you.
B. At the bottom of the sea.
C. A soft bed.
D. Up a tree.
E. Nowhere. I am dead.

What is your favourite food?

A. Whatever you offer me is wrong.
B. Anything that floats past.
C. All food makes me happy! Thank you.
D. Whatever I grub out of a hole in a tree.
E. Nothing. I am dead.

What is your mood right now?

A. Annoyed at you asking me questions.
B. I don't have moods.
C. Super chill thanks for asking, friend.
D. Shy.
E. Nothing. I am dead.

What is your favourite thing about yourself?

A. Everything.
B. I look like a cucumber.
C. I am very loyal.
D. My long thin middle finger.
E. Nothing. I am dead.

What do you like to do at night?

A. Wake up people who are trying to sleep.
B. Not much, same as the daytime.
C. Just sleep and dream.
D. I do everything at night!
E. Nothing. I am dead.

Turn over for the answers...

If you answered mostly As: congratulations, you are a cat. You are a nightmare to live with and you do not care.

If you answered mostly Bs: congratulations, you are a sea cucumber. You have no brain and your head is one big mouth.

If you answered mostly Cs: congratulations, you are a dog. You are a very good boy or girl.

If you answered mostly Ds: congratulations, you are an aye-aye. You are a bit stressful to live with, what with all the jumping around at night but you still behave better than the cat.

If you answered mostly Es: congratulations, you are a dinosaur. You are dead.

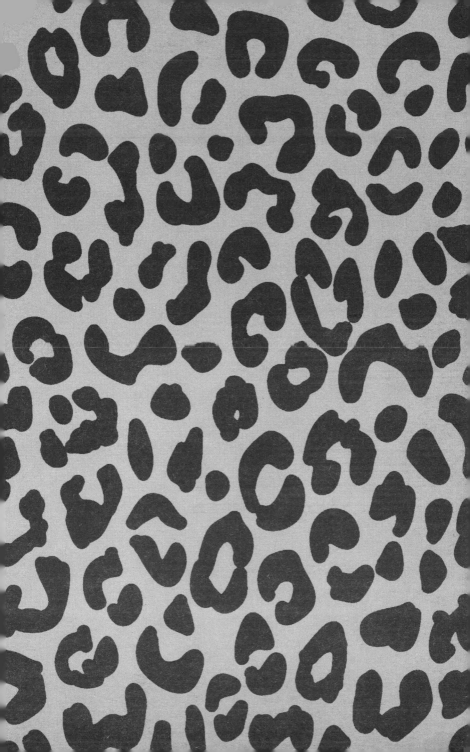